The Village
of
Little Pletzl-
on-the-Zump

OTHER BOOKS BY ALAN L. SIMONS

Eighteen Months- A Love Story Interrupted

The Village of Little Comely-on-the-Marsh

The Children of the Forest

*The Incredible Adventures of Captain
MacDuddyfunk in Cuggermuggerland*

Sweaty Cats and Baby Pigeons

The Village
of
Little Pletzl-
on-the-Zump

Alan L. Simons

BARONEL BOOKS
Toronto

.

This edition is published by Baronel Books,
Toronto, Canada.

First Paperback Edition

Library and Archives Canada Cataloguing in
Publication information is available upon request.

ISBN 978-1-7782137-3-1

http://littlepletzl.com/

littlepletzl@proton.me

DEDICATION

Once again, I thank my wonderful family and friends, who continue to have the patience to put up with my unique sense of humour and style.

The Village of Little Pletzl-on-the-Zump is the sequel to the book *The Village of Little Comely-on-the-Marsh.*

Pletzl, the story, weaves around the lives of a bizarre Yiddish-speaking community of 613 people living for hundreds of years in a small village somewhere in the south of France, exclusively in their own world, without a care or a familiarity with their surroundings. They speak a distinctive Yiddish dialect called Frantsoydish.

Pletzl, in essence, is a clone community, not unlike that of the Welsh community of Comely. Both villages, although close to each other, have no knowledge they both exist, until . . .

The storyline humorously with innate satire and respect addresses cultural diversity fears that go beyond the stereotypes of our society and demonstrates that we can make fun of ourselves, irrespective of where we come from.

ACKNOWLEDGMENTS

Thank you "J" for your support and comments.

Shamelessly, I acknowledge I have attempted to transliterate various common Yiddish expressions into Frantsoydish.

To quote Voltaire, "Woe to the makers of literal translations, who by rendering every word weaken the meaning! It is indeed by so doing that we can say the letter kills and the spirit gives life."

To life!

-1-

SOMEWHERE off of Route D61 in France, near the Village of Little Comely-on-the-Marsh and about five kilometres from La Charce, on the river L'Oule, and about six kilometres from Rottier, all located in the department of Drôme, in southeastern France, lies the extraordinary Village of Little Pletzl-on-the-Zump.

You won't find Little Pletzl-on-the-Zump located on any map. Nor will you find any reference to it in any of the libraries in Valence or Gap. If one has any sense of imagination, and I hope you have, you might establish, on a very good day, its whereabouts, by suggesting Pletzl is in the vicinity of the Château de la Charce.

As you may know, this castle owes its fame to Philis de la Charce, the heroine of Dauphiné. In addition, Le Bistro de Rottier, regarded as a charming little country bistro, for its Rumsteack de boeuf Charlois and the occasional glass of Côtes du Rhône Village, is just four minutes drive south of Rottier.

However, if you were to ask the residents, of La Charce or Rottier communes, with a combined population on a good day of around 62, about Little Pletzl, they probably would deny its existence, mumbling under their breath: "Va te faire cuire un oeuf!" *(Go suck an egg!)*. Or in the common Frantsoydish vernacular, "Gey zukh dem vint in feld." *(Get lost, don't bother me!)*.

You see, for all intent and purposes, Little Pletzl-on-the-Zump is, well, in the wrong place at the wrong time. It shouldn't even exist.

No one living knows for sure how Little Pletzl acquired its name, shortened I might add by some of its older residents to "Plutz". However, as in numerous legendary stories, Little Pletzl had decided many, many years ago, and after some heart rendering arguments at their community's village council meetings, in searching for a name, that their village would be called "Little Pletzl" after their namesake, which is located in the Jewish quarter in the 4th arrondissement of Paris, France.

Yes, and that's Little Pletzl, with its 613 Frantsoydisher-speaking residents, plus one nag, eighteen goats, thirty-six milking cows, seventy-two sheep, and its broiler and layer chicken farm.

But where did the original inhabitants come from? Of course, there were some vague stories, and please correct me if you know I'm wrong, of Maria Theresa Walburga Amalia Christina, the ruler of the Habsburg dominions from 1740 until she died in 1780, insisting her citizens start using surnames. A lot of Yiddish-speaking communities of the time utterly resisted.

But resistance was futile. And over the course of forty years various Yiddish citizens, family by family, group by group, community by community, decided they'd had enough. So, they moved west, seeking out an area of autonomous land where they would be left alone to continue doing whatever Yiddish-speaking people do best.

But this was just idle gossip, handed down, for the most part, from century to century by the surrounding villagers. There it was!

Today, only two of Little Pletzl-on-the-Zump's 613 Frantsoydisher inhabitants speak French or any other foreign language for that matter. To say the least, they're an odd bunch; eccentric is a word that comes to mind. Simply put, they had a state of mind in the middle of rural southern France, to keep to themselves, in seclusion, for literally hundreds of years.

It was rare for any fremder, (*foreigner*) to find the village. Even throughout the many wars fought on French soil, Little Pletzl-on-the-Zump seemed to have missed all the action. Wars came and went; the bagel was invented; schmaltz disappeared from any healthy diet, and so did cholent, the Hungarian variety; major world disasters appeared out of nowhere; Israel became a nation; men landed on the moon; the warming of the planet; France won the World Cup in 1998, and in 2022, Germany lost to Japan, and Argentina lost to Saudi Arabia. And then there was COVID-19 and the Mpox outbreak. Strangely, none seem to affect the village.

And in time, as it was with many isolated communities, the Yiddish they originally spoke, from many areas in Eastern Europe, developed into one unique dialect called Frantsoydish.

Dear reader, in that respect, I must give you a fair warning. I have attempted to transliterate Frantsoydish into an expression you might understand, with a well-meaning translation into English that follows.

The citizens of Little Pletzl-on-the-Zump voted years ago not to have anything to do with their French neighbours. After all, it was French, wasn't it, and as far as telephones, only one existed in the village just outside the distillery and that didn't work, and as for mobiles – forget it! For both were a sheer menace to their way of life.

TODAY surrounding the village pond stands seven primary buildings. The distillery, called Shenken, faces east, towards Jerusalem, on the sunny side.

Directly opposite, an upscale Michelin kosher restaurant - yes, I did say, Michelin - called Potchke Restaurant and Tea Rooms and what would a Frantsoydisher village be without its deli, called Geshmak, which also doubles up as the butchers, dentist, and barbershop.

To the southwest of the distillery, on a plot of land known for its beauty, also facing east, stands The Zelda and Motti Medical Centre. At the time the name was discussed it was clear to many of the village council members that, because of its size and the small population it would serve, it would be more appropriate to call the building a clinic and not a medical centre. However, Zelda and Motti, the humanitarians of blessed memory, who gave a sizable charitable financial gift towards the building, were adamant. They felt their donation and family name were more in keeping with a Medical Centre. As Motti had explained: "Far vos hot Odem un Khave tsugedekt di mayse mit a blat, ven keyner hot zey nit gezen?" *(Why did Adam and Eve cover their business with a leaf if there was nobody to see them?).*

Between Shenken, the distillery, and Geshmak, the deli, stood in all of its architecture splendour, on a tiny hill, overlooking the pond, the Pletzl Pipdówka Shul, named after a region in eastern Poland where many of Pletzl's community originally came from.

And of course, there was a family-owned Chinese restaurant. But more of this establishment a little later. Zemel's Bakery completed the group.

IT would be fair to say the village "Plutz", as the village inhabitants occasionally called it, is more Yiddish than Yiddish. A bastion, of the Revolutionary Yiddish Anthem, *"*In Ale Gasin*" (On Every Road*), is often attributed to the Yiddish anarchists.

But, don't get me wrong! No anarchists are living in Little Pletzl. At least, not to my knowledge. Only a community containing, and I stress here with no disrespect, many citizens who, let us say, are somewhat unique.

Little Pletzl was something from another era, living up to the expectations, traditions, and rituals that no longer existed in their citizens' home countries. Yes, tradition played an essential part in the lives of all living in Little Pletzl-on-the-Zump.

Little Pletzl-on-the-Zump was self-sufficient in every aspect, never needing to introduce anything French into the village, other than the occasional Préalpes-du-Sud. No French veggies, fruit, or meat for them, and indeed no French wine and certainly no potatoes, thank you very much!

So, one asks, are the inhabitants of Little Pletzl-on-the-Zump French citizens of that great magnificent nation? Yes, of course, technically they are French. But not according to its inhabitants, who have no time for the likes of the EU, its trade policies, the parliamentary system of France, French cultural problems, and unemployment. And one can forget the Euro.

Yes, those who live in Little Pletzl know precisely who they are. For the majority, it's still the memory of such currencies as the grosz, pengö, kopiyka, and leu. In any case, no one had ever heard of anyone venturing into Little Pletzl-on-the-Zump, or expressing a wish, god forbid, to leave. That is, until recently. And this, dear reader, is where my vignette begins. ☼

-2-

IT happened quite recently. One early typical Sunday spring morning, in the Village of Little Comely-on-the-Marsh, somewhere in the south of France, where an eccentric Welsh community had lived undetected for hundreds of years, the mist had hardly risen, and the delicious smell of the first Welsh paned o goffi, *(cup of coffee)* had still to be made, a young man by the name of Twm, the son of Mayor Hastings and Mildred, his wife, got on his bicycle and without the knowledge of Felicity his partner, headed out for the first time in his life, to explore the countryside.

He had a mission, which was to seek out the location of his friend Usman the Usman, the only friend he had ever had.

Before Usman returned to his home in Luc-en-

Dios, he had whispered to Twm the vicinity of where he would be staying.

"If you can, find your way to Route D61. I'll be staying for a while at my aunt's cottage. It's located somewhere between La Charce and Rottier. I'm sure you can't miss it!"

Unfortunately for Twm, he missed it! En route, his bike skidded on the slippery road, and in ending up in a ditch, his right leg became entangled in the down tube of his bike.

If you are at all cognizant of this area, you would be aware route D61 isn't known for its abundance of peloton riders or motorists, and not at six-thirty on a misty Sunday spring morning. So, the chances of either a vehicle or a group of bicyclists stopping to assist Twm, or for that matter, a local French farmer, out for his early morning jog before milking his one and only Montbéliarde, were not too encouraging.

As typical of a young man from Little Comely, Twm didn't believe he was too badly hurt, although his right ankle hurt like hell! He assumed no broken bones and other than a few cuts, grazes, some rips in his clothing, and an awful headache, he felt immensely relieved. Saved, would be as far as I might go to express it.

Twm hadn't a clue where he was, although he

remembered seeing a painted sign saying Site géologique de la Charce a few kilometers back. So, grudgingly he decided to start walking. And walk he did! Within the hour, Twm, now trudging through the early morning spring rain, came across an intersection. It was decision time. He thought that he might consider walking straight on, or should he perhaps turn left? What direction was north? For some inexplicable reason, he turned right. He proceeded to walk to the north, in the drizzling rain, along a winding back road that led to absolutely nowhere.

Within thirty minutes, he started to regret his decision. His ankle, now swollen, was throbbing. He was getting cold and thirsty, and he was wet and wanted a coffee. He should have waited until Comely's Welcome Restaurant and Tea Rooms had opened its doors at eight-thirty. Also, the terrain had engulfed his tracks, and his head was beginning to pound even more.

To use a pun, he wondered where this was all heading. Yet, perhaps just by an inner sense of something he sensed, drove him to continue walking.

Stumbling along, feeling hungry and with a pulsing headache, Twm collapsed and sheltered under a large plane tree where he fell into a deep sleep.

"HELLO there! And what's your name then?"

Twm awoke to find himself in a huge bed covered with starched white sheets. The pillows, two of them, flowered in a plethora of vibrant colours and smelt like his grandmother's lavender bush. He faced an open window overlooking a garden of great beauty. His head, still hurting from the accident, had been bound up with a blue and white bandage.

"Hello there! Nu, what's your name?

In front of him, Twm saw two young ladies. At least he thought there were two.

"My name is Frayda, and this is my twin sister Pesha."

Twm looked at them in dismay, for he couldn't understand a word of the language they were speaking. He shrugged his shoulders, closed his eyes, and fell back to sleep.

"Oh dear me," the twins said in unison. "I think we have a goy amongst us."

"You better run right away and tell Mayor Sandek we have a foreigner amid us," said Frayda to Pesha, with an air of no-nonsense authority.

And that, dear reader, is where all once-upon-a-time stories commence.

SOMETIME later, Twm opened his eyes to find himself scrutinized by a gathering of strange people. Most of the men were all in black, had beards and many wore sidelocks. They were intently looking at him with curiosity and suspicion.

"Er hum! My name is Sandek, Mayor of Little Pletzl-on-the-Zump, and this here," he said, pointing to a large rotund lady, flouting an oversize hat and white running shoes, "is my wife, Blume."

Ah, Blume! One could suggest, and with a certain amount of careful diplomacy, Blume could be compared to the Norse warrior woman Lagertha, a woman highly respected on the battlefield.

Sandek, however, had a different way of expressing his relationship with his wife. "Chasuneh hobn nemt a shtundeh, ober far a gantzen leben hot min tsores!" (*Getting married takes an hour, but for a whole lifetime one has troubles!*).

Now, let me say this. For all intent and purpose to help you along with this story, when required I have transliterated the words spoken in Frantsoydish into English.

Mayor Sandek continued by pointing, in no particular order, to the remaining assembly of people.

"These are my three sons, Zindel, Zelig, and Zemel. This is my daughter Zissa. And over there," he pointed with a faint-hearted sigh that everyone in the room acknowledged with a nod of their heads, whilst looking at each other as if to say, yes we know he's a little different, "is my youngest son, Yankele."

Mayor Sandek continued pointing. "Indyk, he's our chief of police." The visually impaired police officer came forward to take a good look at the foreigner in their midst while instructing his police dog Tookhas to sit still.

"Dr. Christin Wójcik is our medical doctor, coroner, and pharmacist. Feyervaser is our distiller and owner of the Shenken, the distillery, and this is his daughter Livna."

Livna smiled and bobbed her head at everyone. She is, what would be called probably the nearest to a modern-day renaissance woman living in Little Pletzl. But she isn't!

The Mayor continued with a wave of his hands. "This here is Yitzhak, he's our legal representative." The Mayor turned to look at the twins. "Ah, yes! You've already met our two wonderful young nurses, Frayda and Pesha," he said blushing with a smile on his face. His wife, Blume, gave him a dirty look. He continued. "This here is Metger, our barber, dentist, butcher, and deli owner."

Police Chief Indyk approached the bed, looked at the Mayor for his approval, and said slowly and loudly, "Du redst Frantsoydish?" (*Do you speak Frantsoydish?*).

Mayor Sandek put his hands to his face. "No, Indyk, whoever he is," pointing his chubby index finger directly at Twm's nose, "Ask him where he comes from!"

"Fun vanen bistu?" *(Where are you from?).*

Twm, figured out incorrectly he had been asked for his name.

"Twm."

Indyk stepped back to address the group standing behind him. "I think he said he comes from Tvm."

Entirely confused, everyone started to talk over each other. *"*Vos is a Tvm*?"* (*What is a Tvm?*) Blume, the Mayor's wife asked. "It's certainly not one of those peculiar French dialects, is it?"

"No, he didn't say he comes from Tvm. He said Twm," corrected Zindel, her son.

"Tvm or Twm, Oy! Wherever he comes from," his mother responded. "He's a goy*!"* (*a non-Jewish person*).

"A goy? Oy vey!" they all said in unison.

"For the time being, let's keep the knowledge of our visitor's presence just to ourselves," said Mayor Sandek, to which all those present nodded their heads in agreement, but knowing there would be no possible way in keeping the news from all the village Pletzlites.

Dr. Wójcik stepped forward. He had one of those expressive looks on his face that only doctors can muster when taking over a situation.

"Now, now. He has to rest. He needs time. He has a nasty bump on his head and a swollen ankle, and he has a raging temperature. He is suffering from TGA, transient global amnesia. Memory loss. Frayda and Pesha will take good care of him."

The twins smiled, looked at each other, and nodded in a way that any intelligent person could figure out there was trouble brewing ahead! With a wave of his hand, Dr. Wójcik steered everyone, other than Frayda and Pesha, out of the room. ☼

THE two girls dressed in their nurses' uniforms weren't precisely the uniforms we know of today. No nurse today while on duty, would wear a long black skirt with white running shoes, and long sleeves. And both of the girls were in full competition mode to see who wore the sharpest outfit. Even in his ill state, Twm recognised this could be something beneficial to his well-being.

Twm's positive thoughts abruptly came to an end as he became dizzy and started to vomit.

It was Dr. Christin Wójcik who immediately attended to the medical centre's only patient.

"No problem young man. Nausea is all part of your condition. It won't last long. Now, we'll get

Nurse Pesha to clean you up, and change you, and she'll get you some fresh bed sheets." The top sheet, on his bed, slipped off onto the floor.

Nurse Pesha was the first one to notice.

"Oh my god!" she screamed. "He's, he's uncircumcised!"

It would seem Twm had begun, in no uncertain manner, to understand the ways of the Village of Little Pletzl-on-the-Zump were very different to his village, the Village of Little Comely-on-the-Marsh.

OVER the next few hours, Twm was visited by members of the Village Council comprising of Mayor Sandek and his five councillors. Yitzhak, the lawyer; Plotnick in charge of buildings; Shprintza, she was the village's business manager; Velvel, finance, health and welfare, and Ackerman, agriculture.

Mayor Sandek, when his wife Blume wasn't following his shadow, was known throughout the village as the foremost authority on learning how to speak one's mind without regard to the consequences. He was also known by the patrons of the Shenken, the distillery, as someone whose total knowledge of the village's practical affairs was below zero. One word summed up Mayor Sandek. Fake! Perhaps that was the reason Indyk had the unenviable task of escorting the Mayor everywhere he went. One could question, in at least today's world, why had Sandek been elected by the vast majority of the village's people. The answer lies somewhere in the well-known Frantsoydish saying, "Der, vas veyst klenster, redt rub." *(He who knows least talks most)*. For as I write these words to you, Little Pletzl-on-the-Zump, by contrast, functions splendidly by the blessed organisational skills of no-nonsense Shprintza, the village business manager extraordinaire! ☼

THE Village Council met once a month on a Monday morning for two hours starting with a healthy kosher breakfast. The Council had a strict agenda. Ninety minutes for breakfast, followed by a 30-minute discussion regarding village business. They were very specific as to the time they took over breakfast. Their breakfast always consisted of pickled herring with black bread, and hardboiled eggs, followed by slices of day-old babka, a sweet braided cake, and a glass of steaming Lithuanian ground coffee.

It was a prime example of a first-class Frantsoydish breakfast feast that certainly had no difficulty lasting for the entire allocated period.

The breakfast, catered by Potchke Restaurant and Tea Rooms, the village's kosher 1-star Michelin establishment, was prepared under the direction of

Chef Glucke. She had taken over the restaurant after the unexpected death of her husband, famed Michelin Chef Nahum, of blessed memory, a man of great girth and a mouth of comparable size, who had died one Friday morning tasting some cooked chicken feet that had become lodged in his throat.

It was said Nahum had a lineage dating back over three hundred years to Rabbi Israel Ben Eliezer, the kabbalist, and healer. Regardless of the Michelin award, this in itself secured his right, by his customers, and now passed down to his wife, to produce an exceptional breakfast cuisine.

Yes, I suspect you're probably wondering, as I was, how the Village of Little Pletzl-on-the-Zump's kosher Potchke Restaurant and Tea Rooms attained Michelin accreditation. For it is certainly not listed in The Michelin Guide. What I can tell you is the village's size had no bearing on it. After all, as you might know, there are other villages located in Europe that have acquired Michelin accreditation. Kruiningen in the Netherlands, Brusaporto in Italy, and Dries, in Germany, come immediately to mind. However, other than Barcelona's Xerta restaurant, Potchke, at the time of writing, is the only other kosher Michelin star location.

One's imagination, and with some degree of resourcefulness, might suggest somehow 18 years ago, on route D61, in a section called Rte de Die, the Michelin logo was obtained by the hands of Potchke's junior partner, none other than Mayor Sandek. Nu! And let's leave it like that!

MAYOR Sandek was the first member of the village council to visit Twm. Dr. Wójcik had set up a rigid visitation schedule. Eight minutes per person. One person at a time, although the rule was waived for the Mayor and Chief of Police Indyk.

Indyk initiated the questioning. "Other than telling us he speaks a language called Twm, has he spoken to you girls?" Frayda and Pesha looked at each other and shook their heads.

Dr. Wójcik, a doctor of the variety known for having passionate integrity for respect, and discretion, intervened. "Mayor Sandek, our young man is in no fit condition to be cross-examined and especially not by…" Dr. Wójcik looked directly into Indyk's only eye. He continued: "And not by Indyk."

Frayda and Pesha continued with their daily chore of nursing, but they knew what Dr. Christin Wójcik meant. Indyk, with the egotism of the Pharisees, wasn't trusting anyone who didn't follow the oral law of the Faith. And now, his suspicions, with the foreigner who spoke Twm, had increased the total to two. For Indyk, two goyim were two too many.

"Yes, yes, yes! I understand. Perhaps we'll return on another occasion. Come, Indyk, time to leave." And with that, a red-faced Mayor Sandek followed by a grunt by Indyk, and a whine from police dog Tookhas said their goodbyes.

TWM, the Twm who spoke Twm, might not have understood the language of these strange people, but he was well-versed in perceiving their body language.

He grew up as a young boy in the Village of Little Comely-on-the-Marsh, The population of 347 religiously followed Welsh Evangelical Methodism.

He was a timid lonely boy, an only child with a dominant mother and a father whose aspirations solely focused on local politics. Twm enjoyed fishing, and often he would walk around Comely's village pond gazing into the water, wondering if he would soon be strong enough to catch a farmed rainbow trout.

It was in Comely that he spent his time observing people. He concluded, quite correctly, not all Welsh Methodists felt empathy towards each other.

Growing up, these experiences helped him grasp what it meant to be a Comely Welsh Methodist, a minority sect that is encouraged to drink wine socially in moderation and believe in reincarnation. ☼

.

5

FROM their earliest infancy, Frayda and Pesha knew they wanted to become nurses, a profession much admired by every boy reaching puberty. All of the twins' appreciation for nursing was confirmed as they became teenagers volunteering at the Potchke Restaurant and Tea Rooms. It was as if nursing found them. Dr. Wójcik was the co-conspirator. While eating a portion of his turkey breast shish kebab, and grilled vegetables on a bed of rice, he had a severe attack of acid reflux.

Sensing the emergency, the twins by instinct, hastily took up the challenge, and with enthusiasm magnificently applied the Heimlich manoeuvre on him.

Although, as they were later told by Dr. Wójcik,

acid reflux and Dr. Heimlich had not the slightest association with each other, it remains a mystery to this day how the twins knew what to do. Still, they came through like champions, to which Dr. Wójcik rewarded them with their lifetime ambition, to become student nurses.

After studying for two years, under the supervision of Dr. Wójcik, he announced they were ready to assist him in his medical practice.

Unbeknown to Twm, the twins' acclaim to nursing was only declared a few hours before he arrived at the medical centre. He was affirmed as their first real live patient and Pesha, with a smile directed at her sister, decided to take control of the situation.

If there was something Nurse Pesha had managed to do, after her outburst in seeing an uncircumcised pots for the first time, it was, if I can offer to freely express it here, was to raise Twm's spirits. For it awakened him from some of his partial loss of memory and was immediately recognised by the two nurses as a sign that he was finally returning to life. It was, however, a sign Twm decided for the most part to keep secret.

"HELLO, anyone here?" Yitzhak's head could be

seen between the centre's two swinging doors. Yitzhak was an unusual character, even by the village's standards. He was a very deaf 91-year-old court jester figure. With one of the best Jewish law and jurisprudence minds in the village who knew everything there was to know about Halakha, the laws derived from the written and Oral Torah, he was called der anderer rebbe, *(the other rabbi)*.

Der ershter rebbe, *(the first rabbi),* Rabbi Dudel ben Shalom was, in name only, the religious leader of the village. Unfortunately, some years ago, outside his home, on a Saturday morning, during the Jewish celebration of Sukkot, he slipped on a piece of Etrog, *(citron)* and injured his back.

Many of his congregants felt the incident was caused by Rabbi Dudel's obsessive feelings of envy of Yitzhak's vast religious knowledge and that a supernatural being, an evil eye, had bewitched the rabbi. And then there were some of his congregants, nay, the majority, who argued that far too much early-morning sweet Frantsoydish wine had been the cause.

An emergency meeting was called by the Board of Governors of Little Pletzl's village shul and in a vote of 17-1, they urged their rabbi to fend off the evil eye and perform the Rosh Hashanah Tashlich ritual in a body of water that contains fish, because it is said fish are incapable of being affected by the evil eye. Rabbi Dudel strenuously refused. "It's absurd! It's too late! We're now in the religious festivity of Sukkot, not the Jewish New Year!"

And with that, Rabbi Dudel ben Shalom said with these words, "Beser a shande in poneem vee a vaitig in boich," (*Better shame in one's face than pain in one's stomach),* stormed out of the board meeting, never to return.

In the meantime, Yitzhak, the anderer rebbe, sadly at the infighting taking place at the village Shul between board members, became agitated and reckless, causing him to have fits of depression, which led him to decide on a career change.

At the age of 91 years, Yitzhak entered a period of self-isolation which resulted in him becoming a self-proclaimed orthodox Jewish guru, the traditional kind, now wearing white clothing, comprising of upper and lower garments with open sandals. A white yarmulke *(a skullcap)* adorned his head, on top of his flowing shoulder-length grey hair.

His mission, as he described it to me, was to become a spiritual vegan advisor to the youth of the village.

He had a companion. A friend by the name of Shprintza, the village business manager. In her youth, she was once regarded as an accomplished four-key bassoonist, known as the most difficult woodwind instrument to master, a musical instrument that requires all ten fingers to play. Regrettably, some years ago, while cutting up some hard cheese, she lost her left index finger to a very sharp kitchen knife.

Needless to say, this incident not only affected her ability to play the bassoon again but for some obscure reason, it affected her vocal cords as well, to the extent her voice began to resonate similar to that of a baritone singer.

Shprintza never left Yitzhak's side, a constant companion. But she had her faults. I wouldn't say she was an alcoholic, god forbid! However, she had the reputation of finishing a large glass of the region's finest wine, made from labrusca grapes, before you could recite the Hebrew blessing for wine.

To those of you who aren't familiar with these oddities, perhaps I ought to explain. Compared to the vast majority of the village population, Yitzhak and Shprintza were quite normal!

But to return to Twm, the Twm who spoke Twm. Yitzhak's interest in the village's foreigner wasn't at least of a curious nature. It was one both Frayda and Pesha saw through instantly. Yitzhak had been sent by Mayor Sandek to infiltrate the medical centre and conduct a soft interrogation on Twm, the Twm who spoke Twm. Yitzhak's companion Shprintza, would act as a decoy.

Yitzhak and Shprintza were given precisely eight minutes by the village's medical team to do what they were best at doing. And for the first seven minutes, all three stared at each other. Twm was particularly intrigued with Yitzhak. Somewhere at the back of his mind, he had the feeling he had met Yitzhak before.

By the time Yitzhak had expressed his first utterance, "Mm, yes hello!" a comment that would have put him in the same category as let us say, a Western Rockhopper penguin casually swimming up to a hungry orca whale, it was time for him and Shprintza to move on to better things. ☼

6

LATER that same morning, created exclusively for Twm by Chef Glucke, of The Potchke Restaurant and Tea Rooms she sent Twm a perfect village old-style Little Pletzl breakfast, now named after her late husband renowned Michelin Chef Nahum, of blessed memory.

"The Nahum" not only consisted of pickled herring with black bread, and hardboiled eggs, followed by slices of day-old babka, and a glass of traditional steaming Lithuanian ground coffee. It also comprised of fried eggs, cucumbers, tomatoes, and feta cheese. It was a sight not easily forgotten and especially not, after hearing about it, from members of the village council.

But what caught Twm's eye, beyond the aroma

and the look of the food, was the indiscrete Potchke Restaurant and Tea Rooms card leaning on the glass of coffee. "(K) Michelin." *(Kosher Michelin)*.

For the second time Twm, the young man from the Village of Little Comely-on-the-Marsh, believed he must have arrived in heaven.

DAYS later, the news of Twm's arrival in the village received much excitement from the younger members of the community, but the complete opposite from its older citizens. They included two of its more, shall we call them, say for the lack of an appropriate term, marginal inhabitants.

For instance, Beynish, the daughter of Plotnick the carpenter and village council member who has the task of overseeing new building projects in the village, and Zon, her husband, the son of Ackerman, the council member with the agriculture portfolio, had taken a vow, on the day of their marriage, to live in an old broken-down barn located on an apple orchard and convert the property into a five-bedroom home, as well as a social entertainment centre, which they named at a well-attended event, Der Glik Tsenter *(The Happiness Centre)*.

In addition, their idea was to manufacture a high-proof liquor called Horinka, a very strong liquor made from a closely-guarded family recipe, and sell it to the centre's customers who played Mahjong and Canasta five and a half days a week.

Strangely, after several financially successful months, Beynish and Zon didn't realise how efficacious their Horinka had become to the married women of Pletzl. And on a dark Sunday evening, two very large buxomly women, in an inebriated state, on their way home and with the joy of winning at Mahjong, accosted none other than Rabbi Dudel.

It would seem the rabbi didn't appreciate their humour of being referred to as the Rabbi Etrog. In doing so he responded to the two ladies with the words, "Nit fun a shaineh tsurkeh vert a guteh veib." *(A pretty face doesn't make a good wife!)*.

Having been personally embarrassed by the rabbi, the two inebriated ladies were not happy, and as they approached him, the rabbi took a step backward, slipped on an empty bottle of Horinka, and fell head face into the pond where he nearly, but not quite, drowned.

Luckily, Beynish and Zon were in the neighbourhood, heard the screaming, and ran to the pond where they, with great effort, managed to pull Rabbi Dudel out of the water.

Beynish and Zon were honoured by the Village

Council for saving the Rabbi and, as they said a few days later, what better way could there be but to initiate a new label for their Horinka by calling it, "The Dudel."

This, in turn, was not appreciated by the Rabbi, who, after his etrog incident, some months earlier, suffered excruciatingly from being a teetotaler.

THE village also had its fair share of what I would call the nearest to be, "perfectly well-balanced citizens". Bear with me here on this! Take for instance the two unmarried sisters, Toltse and Henda. A finer pair of sheep shearers one could only wish to meet. Both of them are also accomplished, musicians. They have run the Little Pletzl Music Friendship Society for fifty-four years. Once a week, on a Tuesday evening, they would invite a small gathering of villagers, of a certain standing, to join them in their music salon to listen to a medley of their eclectic compositions.

Toltse played the zamphona, a strange-looking medieval six-string instrument, while Henda enthusiastically accompanied her sister on a gemshorn, a primitive flute.

Henda had a unique way of welcoming the guests. As they entered her home she would shout to her sister, "Toltse, hide the silver!" Toltse, on the other hand, had the task of bidding the guests goodnight by saying to them, "Thank you for leaving!"

As far as the sisters' sheep shearing experiences; I'll come to this a little later.

To be quite candid, the sisters are nearest to what I can best describe as being typical of Little Pletzl's well-balanced citizens as I'll ever get, or at least want to.

To return to Beynish and Zon, Pletzl's illegal moonshine celebrities.

Beynish concluded, in an argument with her husband, their living quarters in their small converted one-room home, located in the far end corner of their entertainment centre, had better be given some immediate consideration to being enlarged. She was, dear reader, already eight months pregnant.

During the next four and a half years, Beynish, who, as she once described to me, had never wanted to venture outside of the Der Glik Tsenter since her marriage to Zon, was joined by baby number three. With that in mind and weighing 105 kg (232 lbs) and little exercise, other than taking care of her children, Beynish insisted it was time once again to explore their apple orchard, pick some Rozeve Leydiz *(Pink Ladies)*, and become strictly a Fruitarian, accompanied by a sprinkling of seeds and walnuts thrown in.

WITH their marriage vows to each in disarray and their long life five bedroom dreams in ruin, Zon and Beynish took on a whole new different lifestyle. Zon began to drink all of their Horinka profits like a fish and took up smoking a psychoactive drug, for his spiritual development.

Beynish started to spend eighteen hours a day picking and tasting apples, wore the same clothes for months on end, and became the leading village authority of the codling moth, which ate its way through much of the orchard's apples.

Zon, before his marriage to Beynish, had been a very active person, always smiling, in fact probably overactive in his formative years. He had been a keen fitness instructor when younger, but now he had to give it up.

ONE evening, a year ago in June, just after sunset, waiting to watch the full moon rise above the horizon, Zon, after drinking too much Horinka and smoking pot, for his spiritual development, became disoriented. His bicycle hit a rock, and he came off his bike with such a thud that Dr. Wójcik said Zon had severely fractured his tibia in both of his legs. Poor Zon, in bed he suffered terrible bedsores. Over time his physical situation deteriorated, and bacterial contamination and infection set in. Heartbroken, he ended up having both legs amputated and died. But, dear reader, this is the noblest part of the story, with a smile, even on his death bed, he never stopped telling his wife he had experienced not only seeing the largest and most colourful full moon ever, but by some mystical intercession, which he believed he had a hand in, all the codling moths stopped eating the apples, flew in front of the moon, and vanished. A miracle!

In the presence of Rabbi Dudel ben Shalom, Zon, as he struggled to speak his final prayer, Oydoy aoyf a toyt bet (*Confession on a death bed*) before his breath vanished from him, reflecting his love for his wife, held her hand, smiled at her and said, "Beynish, meyn veyb. Men darf nit zein shain – nor chainevdik." *(Beynish, my wife. If you have charm, you don't have to be pretty)*. And with those comforting words to her, Zon died! ☼

.

7

TWM'S next visitor was the extraordinaire full-time non-creative accountant, opera singer Velvel. He arrived, not at Mayor Sandek's bidding, but to audit the medical centre's supplies, as well as to get a private peep of Twm, the Twm who spoke Twm.

Both nurses, Frayda and Pesha, were in love with the gentle giant. Velvel was a huge man measuring some 200 cm tall (79 inches) and weighed in at 125 kg (275 lbs). For that portly figure of a no-nonsense non-creative accountant, the rumour said he was perhaps a distant relative of Velvel Zbarjerin, the famous itinerant singer of yesteryear.

As to his singing, the similarity couldn't be denied. In his early twenties, Velvel had already established himself as a real folksy poet whose songs about the olden days, brought many a tear to his male audience as he sang and danced, in costume, to anyone who would listen to him in the Shenken, Pletzl's distillery.

One song in particular, "Ich hob dich kieb ober fun der veitens, *(I love you from afar),* became a favourite to all the married men quietly having a drink, or two, away from their wives!

EVEN though Velvel was respected and looked up to by the community, he had one slight problem, I'll rephrase that, he had two little problems. He had the smallest feet imaginable for such a giant. Shoe size six (37 European).

Looking up to, well, let's put it into perspective, looking up "at" Velvel was fine and not down towards his kleyn fis *(little feet),* as Twm had done, wasn't the most appropriate thing to do.

POSSIBLY because of language complications, no one had thought of preparing Twm.

Twm was sleeping at the time. Velvel arrived carrying a gift for him of a large steaming bowl of home-made chicken soup, containing carrots, celery, sweet onion, parsnips, and soft matzo balls, but no chicken feet, the likes of which Twm, who spoke Twm, if he never ate another morsel of food again in his life, would have satisfied his appetite.

Unhappily, on waking, Twm had difficulty in expressing an appreciation. Instead, his eight dramatic words were in Welsh, "O fy Nuw! Mae gennych draed mor fach!" translated splendidly into Frantsoydish. *(Oh, my God! You have such small feet!)*.

VELVEL was, at least by character, a gentle giant. Empathetic comes to mind. But if there was one sensitive issue he couldn't handle, it was a comment, about his little feet. And, it was Twm, the Twm who spoke Twm who received the full force of the gentle giant's distress. For no sooner had Twm's expressive remark, in Welsh I might add, been recognised, than an almighty three-hour selection from Wagner's Die Meistersinger von Nürnberg was, in a trice, pronounced by Velvel as a fitting response. In the meantime, Twm gladly accepted and ate the home-made bowl of chicken soup and all of its contents without any remorse for his overt actions.

You see, quite simply put, Twm, coming from a musical Welsh ethnicity background in Little Comely-on-the-Marsh, enjoyed opera, in any language. In fact, he had considered humming the melody, but the chicken soup, with its extraordinary-looking small soft dumpling balls, took precedence.

DURING that day Twm was visited by a steady stream of villagers all wanting to have a peek at Twm who spoke Twm. I, personally, would call it an astonishing encounter, or to perhaps more eloquently quote Dostoevsky who said, "We sometimes encounter people, even perfect strangers, who begin to interest us at first sight, somehow suddenly, all at once, before a word has been spoken."

THERE'S always one or two characters who immediately stand out of the crowd, and this was no exception.

Feyervaser, the owner of Shenken the distillery, was by all accounts, a decent enough fellow. Except he had a serious disorder. He suffered from Anatidaephobia. The fear that all the warty-faced Muscovy Ducks in Little Pletzl's pond, facing the distillery, were continually looking at him.

Sadly, over the years, as more Muscovies joined their waddling friends, Feyervaser's condition became steadily worse. He hardly ventured out of Shenken's front door, the door that faced the pond, and therefore he took his leave, when sober, by climbing out of a back window which made his life somewhat more complicated. You see, the back of the distillery faced an area where friends of the warty-faced Muscovy Ducks, a gaggle of Canada Geese, had elected as their exclusive territory.

Now, what is interesting, as we all know, is the fact that warty-faced Muscovy Ducks are commonly found in central or southern North America, not in the department of Drôme, in southeastern France. The question I'm sure you're asking yourself, as I did, is why are there Muscovies in Little Pletzl?

Well, there are two possible answers. One I obtained from an ornithologist, who suggested some Muscovies might have simply followed a plump of Canada Geese, en route to warmer climes.

The other possibility came from some members of the Pletzl community, who hailed years ago from the Moscow Oblast region of Russia. I have it on good authority they believed the Muscovy must have come from the surrounding area of Moscow proper. Hence the name "Muscovy!"

In my own opinion? That's the way it is!

On the other hand . . . ☼

8

DEAR reader, at this point, I will tell you I have recently noted the abundance of little dogs, all shapes, colours, and sizes residing in Little Pletzl. Let me say, in all honesty, I enjoy the canine animal. Call it what you wish, pooch, doggy, pet, or simply hund!

I mention these details because astonishingly as it seems, Pletzl's little dogs do not walk. They are held under their owner's left armpit and it would seem by the happiness expressed in their eyes, they are quite comfortable in this position.

It seems the term "walkies" has a very different meaning in Pletzl.

Take, for instance, Malvina and Kini, two ladies

also known by their Frantsoydish stage names, Jennya and Hessye, the names I will now address them.

Every day, except Saturday, at eleven in the morning they can both be seen together, with their little pooches held tightly under their left armpits, heading towards Zemel's Bakery for a coffee and a shared slice of spicy and sweet tzimmes cake.

Like many thespians who incessantly love to talk, Jennya and Hessye acted in character on and off the stage. Jennya, the smaller of the two, wore huge platform shoes to compensate for her lack of height. Together with a pair of large dark sunglasses, a bright yellow jacket, and skin-tight black leggings, she looked the epitome of someone who had great difficulty in rising - forgive the pun - to an age which I will go no further in explaining.

There is no use in pretending about it, Hessye was the quieter of the two. She didn't have much of a choice. For most of her conversation with Jennya, she was relegated to simply nodding her head. There is no doubt Hessye was the understudy of this twosome, on and off the stage. As to the two pooches, I never once heard their owners calling them by name. They sat there communicating in a silent language to each other, eye-to-eye, snout-to-snout, looking bored stiff!

A word, or two about Zemel's Bakery. There is no doubt ZB, as it is known by Pletzl's younger community, receives the centre of attention for first and second dating experiences. That is after they have gone through a series of cross-examinations by Pletzl's registered Shadchanit. *(Matchmaker)*.

Faigel was, up to recently, the quintessential certified matchmaker. She made things happen. Her infinite wisdom was regarded with the utmost respect by young Pletzlites and their parents alike. She was one of the principals and influential members of the community. Let me say here, her record of success, was second to none. Faigel abounded with enthusiasm and energy that would put Eliezer, the servant of Abraham, the matchmaker for Abraham's son Isaac, relegated to the second choice.

Regrettably, it saddens me to mention these aforementioned details. The combination of religion in politics is not a subject treated with respect by Faigel. As the exclusive certified Pletzl matchmaker, it was her sworn duty to uphold the primary tenet of her trade. Thou must not be a Yenta! *(A busybody)*.

The point is Faigel, as she became older, became a blabbermouth extreme. Her unrestrained views on how Little Pletzl was run by its village council exceeded the bounds of good breeding. She started to wear a red shawl with the letters MLPGA boldly inscribed around her shoulders. "Make Little Pletzl Great Again," became her mantra. She was decertified as a Shadchanit soon after.

TO continue. And then there was the widow Hannale. A supreme advocate of the roll-your-own cigarette and gambling fraternity. A combination that can only be called an addiction of the highest standards. There was never a time she was observed without a cigarette dangling out of her mouth, supplemented by the ash on her enormous natural H-cup breasts which, with a brush of her right hand, eventually found its way down to her tiny waist.

She was proud of her tiny waist was Hannale. So much so that at all Little Pletzl simchas *(joyous events)* it became a tradition to tell the story about Hannale's tiny waist.

AT the wedding of Beynish, the daughter of Plotnick the carpenter, and Zon, the son of Ackerman the ploughman, Hannale sat, as was the Little Pletzl custom, at a round table for eight with her family. The family, in this case, consisted of her sister Malka, her brother-in-law Wolf, her two brothers, Izik and Jakub, and her two great nieces and one great nephew. By Little Pletzl's standards, it wasn't a particularly dysfunctional family, other than to say the common strain between the eight, regardless of where they were, consisted of shouting and arguing at each other, at full strength, over the slightest issue.

Well, to continue. As the story goes. While the group of eight were eating their stuffed roasted chicken, accompanied by a medley of home-grown Pletzl vegetables and potatoes, Hannale, with her mouth full of food, keeled over and ended up with her face in the medley. As to the roasted chicken, it found its way temporarily assigned between her H-cups.

Thankfully, after a much-animated discussion on what to do, Hannale's two nieces managed to guide her to the nearest female-friendly toilet, where they cleaned her up and diagnosed the problem. Hannale's under bust corset was too tight.

The two nieces, guided by the principles of decency, said nothing on their return to the table. On the other hand, they removed the table's centrepiece of fresh flowers and in its place, with a flourish, deposited Hannale's corset.

Hannale, in front of all the wedding guests, standing erect, flouting her H-cups and her tiny waist, with a roll-your-own cigarette now dangling out of her mouth, responded magnificently.

"De pave zol nit hobn di sheyne federn, volt zikh keyner a fir nit umgekukt!" *(If the peacock didn't have beautiful feathers, no one would pay any attention to it).*

From that day, the story about Hannale and her corset was told at every Little Pletzl simcha *(joyous)* event. ☼

9

WHAT would a Yiddish community living in France, whose citizens spoke Frantsoydish, be without a Chinese restaurant owned by the Zhōu family, who spoke Hokkien, whose roots, generations ago, came from Puyuan Village in Fujian Province, southeastern China?

Puyuan Village. It has been written, "Over eight centuries, Puyuan residents lived in harmony with the carp, so much so, rules were made to protect the carp including the preparation of funeral rituals and burial places for deceased carp."

But not for this Zhōu family, who were looking for an opportunity to better themselves. And better themselves they did!

Jewish merchants and traders of that time visiting Puyuan Village told stories of groups of Jews leaving their communities in Eastern Europe and were heading west for a healthier and safer life.

Just by chance, a Jewish merchant asked a villager for their name. The Puyuan resident replied "Zhōu." To which tears came into the eyes of the merchant. Fearing he had offended the Jew, the villager asked why he was crying.

"We are family!" the merchant replied. What he wasn't aware of was the name Zhōu in the villager's dialect is pronounced "Jew."

"You are mishpocha! *(family)* and look," he said pointing down at the 3,000-meter-long Carp Brook, "And you have carp?"

In seconds, the Zhōu family realised their future was secure.

Today, the descendants of the original Zhōu family are upstanding community members of Little Pletzl. Other than a slight Hokkien Chinese accent, their Frantsoydish is as good as their neighbours. And their fish and vegetarian restaurant caters to a clientele anyone would be proud of, especially on December 25.

On this day, the Zhōu Family Restaurant, in

THE VILLAGE OF LITTLE PLETZL-ON-THE-ZUMP

keeping with tradition, has a set menu consisting of:

Crispy Spring Rolls
Stir-Fried Garden Fresh Mixed Vegetables

Deep-Fried Filet of Sole
or
Steamed Salmon with Black Bean Sauce or
Fresh Lemon Sauce

Mixed Vegetable Fried Rice
or
Steamed Rice

Deep-Fried Banana with Ice Cream
or
Mango Pudding

-10-

AT this point in my story, I pause and perhaps I should, for the sake of clarity, take full responsibility and apologise for deviating from telling you more about Twm, who speaks Twm.

In past generations, I suppose I would have been called bird brain, or at least referred to with the term "Hok a chanik." *(a chatterbox!).*

However, I recently learned the part of my brain associated with intelligent behaviour is front-loaded with far more neurons than I had been given credit for.

To return to Twm. I recall distinctly Twm was visited by a steady stream of villagers all wanting to have a peek at him, a curiosity, or just to pay their respects. I, personally, would call it an extraordinary happenchance.

And that, dear reader, I recollect is what happened. For Twm who, when he saw the collection of Frantsoydishers walking past him, had doubts if he was alive. It vaguely reminded him of the times in his Welsh village of Little Comely-on-the-Marsh, of the Chapel of Rest where one's friends and loved ones paid their final respects before the funeral service.

For here he was in bed, enclosed with the whitest starched sheets imaginable, facing a window overlooking the most unbelievable beautiful flora, with a steady stream of Pletzl visitors, one-by-one, quietly walking past him, also reminded him of his Comely friend Usman, the Usman, who spoke Usman.

Twm remembered the time in Comely he was sitting below a similar window, facing Usman, who was in a hospital bed, not unlike the one he was currently in. However, right now it was Yankele, the son of Mayor Pletzl, who had taken a similar position. It was as if he, Twm, had lived through the present situation before today.

ALL of this fascination with past events was broken up by the arrival of Dr. Cristian Wójcik who immediately, as one would expect, took control of the situation.

"This is a medical centre. If you have been diagnosed with dysphoria, insomnia, or fatigue, please leave the premises right now and go and make an appointment with Rabbi Dudel."

In a wink of an eye, the Zelda and Motti Medical Centre became a deserted wilderness.

DURING the ensuing days, Twm took all the comings and goings in his stride. His decision to keep quiet by not uttering a single word had reaped benefits for him, and he was hesitant to change this arrangement. However, the dilemma he faced was he wanted to sustain the patient-nurse relationship as long as possible. Yet, such a mirage of deception was becoming more and more difficult. He felt caged in bed, unable to walk, and his smiles - and what smiles they were, to nurses Frayda and Pesha, now included him raising his thick eyebrows up and down, which were quickly translated by the twins.

The twins saw his non-verbal language skills as a sign of an impending change in their relationship with him, and they prepared to pounce upon it at the earliest possible occasion. Yet, for Frayda and Pesha the attraction to unknown possibilities resulted in them remembering what their Oma, of blessed memory, had once a month emphasized to them. "Az men zetst a feygele in shtaygele arayn, veys men nit tsi lakht es tsi veynt es. *(When you put a bird in a cage, you don't know whether it's laughing or crying).*

All of these goings-on were quietly observed by Yankele, the son of Mayor Sandek, who sat under the window facing Twm.

YANKELE, now approaching his 19th birthday, felt secure sitting cross-legged facing the two beds, one occupied for the first time, in the medical centre's in-patient facility. It was his regular place where he could withdraw from the world of his siblings and parents and not be hindered by the daily squabbling and infighting occurring between members of his family.

He knew from an early age he was, somehow, just different, he had overheard Dr. Cristian Wójcik explain to his parents he was a socially anxious introvert, whatever that meant!

No doubt some of this was fueled by the fact he was not only the youngest of his four siblings, but, there was an age difference of 24 years between Zilig, the oldest, and himself. The boys Zilig, Zemel, Zindel, and his sister Zissa were always reminding him he was a "Teus fun din," *(an error of judgement)*.

Over time, as a teenager, he established a nonverbal means of communicating, mostly with a nod of his head or a shrug of his shoulders. Conversation at home on topics such as Torah and Talmud and religious texts didn't interest him. He was engrossed in dendrology and silvology, the scientific study of trees, and the understanding of natural forest ecosystems surrounding Little Pletzl. His siblings regarded him as being "Avek di vant" *(Off the wall!)*.

"Perhaps, before he gets married, he'll grow out of it. It's probably a stage in his life. I wish he had more friends his age," Mayor Sandek would repeatedly say to his wife.

"Maybe we should consider getting a second opinion?" Blume, his wife would reply.

"A second opinion? With who? Have you forgotten Wójcik is the only medical doctor we have in the village?" reacted the Mayor.

"Yes, I know! But, you know what I mean, Wójcik, he's really not one of us, is he, and he doesn't understand our customs and culture from the old country. Maybe we should consult Rabbi Dudel?"

"What! That yappy schnoodle? No son of mine is going to be …"

And with those final words, the matter came to an abrupt end. ☼

11

THE Little Pletzl Married Ladies & Widowers Circle to say is a lively group intended for the contemporary Jewish women of Pletzl, is somewhat of a parody.

Yes, it does deliver original and inspiring actions, including a vast assortment of hands-on activities, discussions, workshops, delicacies to taste, and unwavering fun.

I would say, and correctly me if I'm wrong, their slogan is best described as being engaging and impacting the community through relevant and meaningful programs providing, at the least, heated discussion on how to select the next debate topic that has a solid argument potential.

However, in keeping with their traditional

values, certain topics are not recognised as being appropriate. These include: Sex work should be legal; all people should be vegetarians; humans should invest in technology to explore and colonize other planets, and human cloning should be permitted.

Nevertheless, all of these, one would call debatable topics in other societies, were put aside with the arrival of the first goy in generations. Twm.

At an all-day emergency committee meeting, the Little Pletzl Married Ladies & Widowers Circle decided, by finally a unanimous vote taken late in the evening, it was their duty to take Twm, if I may use some discretion here, to take him under their wing. And what better way was there than to express it through the culinary delights of their community.

After all, to quote from the widow Riva who said, "Alts ken der mentsh fargesn nor nit esn." *(A person can forget everything but eating)*. And so it was.

DIRECTLY facing Yankele, Twm's bed, now festooned with a selection of beetroot soup; brisket; cholent, a slow-cooked stew of meat, potatoes, beans, and barley; Holishkes, stuffed cabbage with rice and meat, baked with tomatoes; Kugel, baked sweet casserole made of noodles with vegetables and fruits; Tzimmes, a sweet stew of carrots and yams with raisins; Helzel, stuffed poultry neck skin; Gedempte fleisch, pot roast, with beef, vegetables, tomato paste, and spices; and Vareniki, filled dumplings.

It was Twm who took the first step. He gestured for Yankele to join him to share in the food he had received from his admiring ladies. It was an offer Yankele could not refuse. Both of them, in perfect harmony, sat in silence overwhelmed by the extent of the variety. It reminded me of the movements of a symphony. First, the allegro, followed by the adagio, the minuet, and finally the rondo. All are in perfect order. Mission accomplished!

Yankele felt he owed his new-found friend a sign of his gratitude.

WHAT happened after that would in time be written up in Pletzl's historical records. Yankele spoke. Not a shrug. Not a facial acknowledgement. Two words. "Thank you!" The significance of the event could be compared to Piotr Ilich Tchaikovsky taking it upon himself to personally fire the five cannon shots in his 1812 Overture.

DURING the ensuring days Twm's and Yankele's friendship nurtured. With Dr. Wójcik's approval, Yankele was allowed to occasionally take Twm out of the Zelda and Motti Medical Centre in a wheelchair to various highlight spots in the village. Their language barrier put off neither of them, for it showed, with credible evidence, friendships can overcome such simple obstacles as Twm's Welsh language and Yankele's Frantsoydish. For, as any philologist would clearly explain to you, neither of the two characters understood one iota of what they were each saying to the other! The issue was further compounded by the fact Yankele, after years of remaining silent, had only recently decided to speak again.

For Yankele, the brother of Zilig, Zindel, Zemel, and Zissa the son of Mayor Sandek and Mrs. Blume, it meant he had finally found a real friend he could communicate with, without being discouraged by his parents or his siblings who thought him to be dumb and stupid. ☼

12

PIPIDÓWKA Pletzl Shul stands on a little hill overlooking the pond. Built of pine, oak, and beech trees from the forests surrounding Little Pletzl, the Shul is a mastermind of architecture, both externally and internally. The tiered, sloping two-storey roof towers and distinguishes itself superbly over the rooftops of the surrounding buildings.

The Shul also doubles up as the Village Community Centre. The property bustles with life and activity and is used for religious and social activities throughout the day.

The Zelda and Motti Playhouse, a small but well-equipped 189-seat theatre, is accessible through the Shul's side entrance.

The Shul building is blessed by a secular school commonly known by its young students as "The Pipi," much to the dismay of its head teacher, Rabbi Dudel, who also doubles up three days a week as Pipi's Executive Social Director.

I recall distinctly the time the Zhōu family announced to their neighbours that their young children on hearing the name of their school couldn't stop laughing. Pipi in a Chinese dialect means fart!

If there's one mystery prevailing in the village, it has been the complexity between the traditional Yiddish values from the old country you may have read about, and that of Frantsoydisher Pletzl today, a village not only isolated by their own choice from the surrounding French society but perhaps more importantly to you, Pletzl's decision to insulate themselves from other Jews.

As confounding as it must seem to an outsider, the subject bears no relevance to Pletzl's inhabitants. And if you, the reader, were to ask me to respond on behalf of Pletzl, I would simply quote Livna, the daughter of Feyervaser. "What is, is and what will be, be!"

THE Zelda and Motti Playhouse's building, a small, but for Zelda and Motti, a tolerable replica of

Odessa's famous Opera House, was the jewel of Little Pletzl's community. Ferdinand Fellner and Hermann Helmer, the brilliant architects who designed the Odessa Opera House, would have been shaken to see what Little Pletzl had accomplished.

It must be said Fellner and Helmer did not produce typical designs. Each theatre was regarded as being unique, one of a kind. None were identical to the other. And then entered Zelda's and Motti's 189-seat wooden facility.

Its walls were not covered by stucco ornaments with fine gilding. Nor were the seats softened by red tones. The ceiling was not painted by a famous painter representing celebrated satirical episodes from Joseph Zabara's works.

But to all those living in Little Pletzl, their Playhouse was utterly luxurious. Splendid and more important, the seats were warm to their buttocks on a cold evening.

IT was a cold winter evening. The Playhouse was buzzing with excitement. The audience waited in anticipation to hear Goldfaden's successful operetta *The Intrigue,* sung in part and for the first time in Frantsoydish, by their very own songbird and prima donna, Jennya aka Malvina. You may remember her from Zemel's Bakery.

Jennya, without any form of exaggeration, stood out from the crowd. With her huge platform shoes to compensate for her lack of height, her pair of large dark sunglasses, bright yellow jacket, and skin-tight black leggings, together, with her little yappy white pooch held tightly under her left armpit, there was no doubt that Jennya, at some early age in her career, and at another place, might have well received a resounding interest from Henech Kon or Boris Thomashefsky or even Avrom Goldfaden himself. But this was Little Pletzl, not Łódź or Ositniashke or Starokostyantyniv.

Jennya, Little Pletzl's own songbird, and prima donna had, in her long life, become engaged on numerous occasions. However, marriage was not for her. As she openly admitted to anyone in ear-shot: "Beser tsereisen die t'noi'eem aider die ketubah" *(It's better to break off an engagement than to cancel the marriage contract).*

Goldfaden's *The Intrigue* was an enormous success. And, as in his original production, Jennya was given the opportunity to sing a song Goldfaden had borrowed from Le Cocq's operetta, *The Daughter from Hell,* about the romantic exploits of Clairette, a young Parisian florist. She, dear reader, sang it with such utter conviction and passion and an honesty which Velvel described to friends as giving him more depth and meaning to the words, "Ich hob dich hald, nur mein fei'er eriz opgekilt!" *(I love you so, but my fire has cooled off!)* ☼

13

COMMUNITY ball games for seniors were an integral part of life for many of Pletzl's citizens. It was said the game of Pökelpiłka was originally created by Yiddish-speaking seniors hundreds of years ago in the old country. They had become bored and lethargic with their solitary unfulfilled lifestyle. All their children and grandchildren had moved away from the family home. No one connected with them or visited them anymore. Social isolation set in, and all which was left were groups of Omas and Opas who sat facing each other at the local eating house nibbling on their favourite snack, the kosher dill pickle.

What was needed, as the grandparents discussed their situation, was something to keep them socially and cognitively engaged.

"Besides eating kosher dill pickles we need to create a game to challenge our physical and mental condition," remarked one Opa. "Perhaps a ball game?" he added.

Over several months and with much trial, error, and of course argument, the seniors developed a ball game that in essence helped to improve their sense of purpose.

One creative Oma came up with a suitable name for the game. "Pökel", is derived from the German meaning salt and brine, and "Piłka", from the Polish word meaning ball.

Little Pletzl's Pökelpiłka, as it became known - you dear reader, might know it by its English name, "Pickleball", spread throughout the Yiddish-speaking eastern European communities and as the population spread westward, leagues and associations were formed in many cities.

Years later, one such league, exclusively for seniors, was established in Little Pletzl, where Pökelpiłka became the national sport of the village. Teams were formed through the auspices of the Little Pletzl Pökelpiłka Players Association and four indoor courts under one roof were built through a sizable donation, accompanied by a surrounding landscape. And for the first time in history, the courts were designated and named as having first-gender pronouns. Signs never seen before were installed. She/her/hers and he/him/his became the norm.

The structure was called The Zelda and Motti Pökelpiłka Sports Park. It gracefully faced the Pipidówka Pletzl Shul and the Zelda and Motti Playhouse. ☼

14

WHILE Twm, who spoke Twm, was sharing the final vestiges of his delicious baked sweet casserole made of noodles with vegetables and fruits, with his new-found friend Yankele, which had been magnificently prepared by the Little Pletzl Married Ladies & Widowers Circle, an extraordinary in-camera meeting of members of the Village Council was taking place at the Potchke Restaurant and Tea Rooms. Those in attendance included Mayor Sandek and his five councillors. Yitzhak, the lawyer; Plotnick in charge of buildings; Shprintza, the village's business manager; Velvel, finance, health & welfare, and Ackerman, agriculture.

That afternoon there was only one item on their

agenda. Namely Twm and what to do about him.

Perhaps it was just as well the meeting was in-camera, for the suggestions made, so I understand, and let me be very clear here, weren't favourably inclined towards Twm staying longer than yesterday.

As they all sat around the table, slurping on their glass of steaming Lithuanian ground coffee, it was Mayor Sandek, while gazing out of the window looking at the Muscovy Ducks paddling peacefully in the Pletzl pond, who initiated the first thoughtful comment of the day: "Vayl dos lebl broyt iz kaylekhdik, geyen derfar di katshkes borves." *(Because a loaf of bread is round, therefore the ducks go barefoot).*

I can honestly say, if Kant, Mendelssohn, or Buber would have witnessed such a profound opinion, they would have been the first to recommend Sandek to some higher place of authority. Be as it may, none of those physically present had a clue what Sandek was talking about. And neither did he!

I mention these details to give you an appreciation of the dilemma facing Pletzl's Village Council. Elections were coming up in a few months and no civilized member of Council was willing to give up their weekly breakfast, catered by Mrs. Glucke of the Potchke Restaurant and Tea Rooms, the village's kosher 1-star Michelin establishment.

It was Yitzhak, the former lawyer, and der anderer rebbe, *(the other rabbi)* who now, as a self-proclaimed orthodox Jewish guru, decked out in his white clothing, comprising of upper and lower garments with sandals, and a white yarmulke *(a skullcap)* adorning his head, arose from his chair to address his coffee slurping quagmire of colleagues.

"Exodus 22:22 states, 'You shall not wrong nor oppress the stranger, for you were strangers in the Land of Egypt.'"

It was Ackerman who responded with a sarcastic snigger. "Thank you, Yitzhak, or perhaps you would prefer I call you by your newly appointed Guru name, Gurdayal the Compassionate."

Yitzhak took no time to respond. While looking at all his council colleagues, he shook his finger at Ackerman. "Ven er iz tsvey mol azoy klug, volt er geven a goylem." *(If he were twice as smart, he'd be an idiot!).*

Mrs. Glucke couldn't have come in at a better time. "You all better go over to the Medical Centre, there's a bunch of angry protestors led by the Mayor's wife demonstrating against the goy. Dr. Wójcik has locked the doors." She looked at Mayor Sandek. "Your son Yankele is inside with the Twm."

BY the time Mayor Sandek and his five councillors, Yitzhak, the lawyer, also now known as Gurdayal the Compassionate; Plotnick in charge of buildings; Shprintza, the village business manager; Velvel, finance, health & welfare, and Ackerman, agriculture, had ridden their bicycles at furious speed around the Little Pletzl pond to the Medical Centre, an opposing group, the Little Pletzl Married Ladies & Widowers Circle, led by the widow Beynish, the wife of the late Zon, in support of the goy Twm, had formed facing the demonstrators.

Not to be outdone, Blume, the Mayor's wife, had the backing of The Little Pletzl Music Friendship Society, led by Toltse and Henda, the unmarried sisters.

Between them, trying to keep a resemblance of order, Police Chief Indyk and his police dog Tookhas and Rabbi Dudel ben Shalom heroically faced the two groups.

Inside the Zena and Motti Medical Centre peering out of the window, in utter bewilderment, were Dr. Wójcik, his two nurses Frayda and Pesha, Twm, and Yankele.

I would if I had been asked, at first glance compared it to a precursor clash between a combination of Socialists, Communists, and Greens disagreeing with France's far-right National Rally political party.

As the members of the Village Council looked on in confusion, it was Gurdayal the Compassionate who stepped forward between the two opposing sides. He raised his hands high in the air and said with tears in his eyes, "As Paramahansa Yogananda has said, Learn to be calm and you will always be happy."

A hush enveloped both groups. Toltse approached Gurdayal the Compassionate. In her left hand, she carried her priceless zamphona medieval six-string instrument, while her right hand offered Gurdayal an off-white clean facial tissue.

Unfortunately, as they reached out to offer each other's extended hands, they both slipped. Gurdayal landed faced down on some Pletzl zump, while Toltse fell on her priceless zamphona.

No cinematographer could have accomplished such a visual effect as what I witnessed above. Nor could a screenwriter produce such emotional words that Toltse could express, nay screamed, directly at Gurdayal the Compassionate. "Lign in drerd un bakn beygl!" *(May you lie in the ground and bake bagels)*.

Dear reader, it was for Little Pletzl citizens, a curse of all curses. A curse that went beyond all social and cultural boundaries. A curse unheard of for generations. A curse implying you should burn in hell for all eternity and bake bagels you may never eat.

But, there's more to this story that I'm now going to reveal to you.

Up to recently Toltse, the sheep-shearing musician and now the former zamphona player and, as well as co-sponsor of The Little Pletzl Music Friendship Society, and Yitzhak the very deaf 91-year-old court jester figure, with one of the best Jewish law and jurisprudence minds in the village, who knew everything there was to know about Halakha, the laws derived from the written and Oral Torah, who was called der anderer rebbe, *(the other rabbi),* and now also known by his self-proclaimed Jewish guru name of Gurdayal the Compassionate, had at one time been Toltse's lover.

I realize this method of introducing a subject to you is not in keeping with traditional Frantsoydish-Pletzl values. However, since I have openly made a public explanation of Toltse's emotional outburst, I must now offer you how these sordid details came about. ☼

HUNDREDS of years ago, Toltse's and Henda's ancestors lived in an area called Lower Silesia, located in southern Poland. The girls, as they grew up in Little Pletzl, were happy and inquisitive siblings, with a deep passion for music as well as family history. At a young age, their parents obliged them with stories about bygone days. One recurring story, in particular, became their favourite.

The story and we have no reason to dispute it, is related to members of their family being involved in raising sheep. Not just any run-of-the-mill sheep, but Wrzosówkas, the oldest native sheep breed in Poland.

The story fascinated the young girls, and as they

grew up they vowed to become sheep shearers. Luck was on their side. One early spring sunny afternoon, while on their walk among Little Pletzl's bushes and shrubs they came across a small flock of lost Préalpes-du-Sud sheep wandering aimlessly in front of them. Without any consequences of the laws governing the stealing of sheep, they somehow steered the sheep and…

Dear reader, I break here. I am beginning to sense there's no real validity in continuing with the content of this story. For there's no use pretending, I am at a loss. I have to admit I know nothing about sheep, and I mean nothing. Nor can I distinguish the difference between a Préalpes-du-Sud from an Arles Merinos breed, which originally would have been an integral part of this story.

What I will say to you with the utmost sincerity is this: I am sure both Toltse and her sister Henda in another place and time, would have had a good chance of becoming Golden Shears World Sheep Shearing and Wool Handling Champions. But, as of now, at the grown-up age of 88 and 86 respectfully, they just have to contend with being the only sheep shearers in Little Pletzl and in addition, try to make the best of repairing Toltse's priceless zamphona.

And as for Toltse and her emotional outburst against Gurdayal the Compassionate? Perhaps she should take heed of the following proverb: "Az men makht dos moyl nit oyf flit keyn flig nit arayn." *(If you don't open your mouth, a fly won't get in).*

That being said, all those present at the confrontation were so aghast at hearing Toltse's outburst, they packed up and went home.

It is as it is! ☼

16

PIPIDÓWKA Pletzl Shul's Board of Governors consisted of the President, Executive Officers, and Board Members. In addition, there were over eighteen committee chairs including Youth, Cemetery, Medical, Membership, Adult Education, Culture and Entertainment, and so on.

Many years ago, the Board, to provide leadership to the community, made what they thought to be an intelligent decision. They decided to delegate as many people to each committee as possible. And for their service, they would be given free shul membership.

It wasn't until one astute board member, by the name of Metger, months later announced all-in-all, 613 individuals had signed up, the entire number of

Little Pletzl's population. The names of all the adults, the youth, and young children were on the list, including Dr. Christin Wójcik.

Following the convention incurred in many shuls to this day, Pipidówka Pletzl Shul's President and Executive Officers were forced to resign en masse. Bedlam reigned supreme!

IN time-honoured tradition it was Metger, Little Pletzl's exemplary barber, dentist, butcher, and deli owner, who rallied the troops and took control. A man, amongst other things, who had considerable personality and taste. A man who knew everything about dentistry from abrasion to xerostomia. A man who, as a butcher, knew the whole shebang from adjusted backfat thickness to yearling mutton.

He was aided at the time by Co-President Livna, the tasteful 54-year-old unmarried daughter of Feyervaser, the distillery owner.

AH! Livna. Years ago, in her early twenties, buxom, healthy, and plump, she had been approached by Little Pletzl's very own Faigel, the now former registered Shadchanit (*the Matchmaker*). Faigel had a nice boy in mind for her, none other than Metger who was in training to become a barber, dentist, and butcher, (the deli came much later in his life).

Livna, at first was reluctant to meet him, However, after much discussion, she finally agreed, but on her terms.

"I agree to meet him for 30 minutes. We shall sit on a barrel at the back door of my father's distillery amongst the Canada Geese. For the whole 30 minutes, we shall not speak. We shall just kiss. On this basis, I will evaluate his potential for a further meeting."

Dear reader, I have been assured by Faigel herself that is exactly, (word-for-word), what Livna demanded. In addition, Faigel recalls Livna adding the following words of encouragement she was directed to deliver to Metger. "Fun leydike feser iz der lyarem greser." *(Empty barrels make the most noise).*

I am sorry to say, to the disappointment of both of their parents, no further meeting took place between the young buxom and healthy plump Livna and Metger in training, neither in front of the Canada Geese or the warty-faced Muscovy Ducks.

TODAY, Livna is part-owner of Shenken, the

distillery her father, Feyervaser built. Yes, he continues to suffer from Anatidaephobia. The fear of all the warty-faced Muscovy Ducks in Little Pletzl's pond, facing the distillery, continue to look at him. He has become a recluse and only finds joy in chatting with his close friends, over a drink, about the olden days.

He tried to include Livna in the conversations but, she acquired a vocabulary beyond the linguistic ability of many of Shenken's frequent patrons and thus felt rejected by the customers.

The scenario could be well described in one of Jacob Gordin's plays. Gordin. The Yiddish playwright and journalist. Gordin. Who splendidly revolutionized Yiddish theatre.

I mention these details because if Gordin had met our lovely Livna of Little Pletzl he would, I'm sure, have written a great melodrama role exclusively for her.

To return to Metger. He never got married. Other than his multi-businesses, he devoted himself, much to the demise of his social life, as the undisputed life-long president and treasurer of the Little Pletzl Pipidówka Shul and its community. He successfully brought in strong rules that gave him more power to veto certain of the board of governors' approvals, much to the annoyance of his board. As one of them was overheard saying, "Metger's opened the gates of heaven so wide even the angels Michael, Gabriel, Uriel, and Raphael together would have difficulty in crowd control."

However, there was one thing both the president, his board and Rabbi Dudel agreed on. Yitzhak the lawyer and anderer rebbe, aka Gurdayal the Compassionate, would be prohibited from attending any of the shul's activities dressed in white clothing as a self-proclaimed orthodox Jewish guru.

There is no doubt the prohibition caused so much dismay within Pletzl's younger generation, after all, Gurdayal the Compassionate had become their spiritual vegan advisor and mentor, they immediately initiated a group to form a separate religious community and a yoga centre. Metger and his merry band were taken by surprise at the speed at which the youth had started the process.

As one of the youth quite aptly said to Metger, "When you're running from a burning house, you don't stop to kiss the mezuzah." ☼

17

ZEMEL'S Bakery, known within the community as "Zee Bee," was owned by Zemel and his wife Zlata. Zemel was Mayor Sandek's son. Zee Bee was located between Potchke Restaurant and Tea Rooms and the Khōu Chinese Restaurant, on the opposite side of the Pletzl pond facing the Shenken distillery.

Zee Bee was more than a bakery. It only served dairy meals. From early morning to early evening it was the community meeting place. The word heymisher (*cosy*) comes to mind. It was a place full of characters where it was the custom who could talk the loudest. Everyone competed with each other, vying to be heard. And heard they were. Zee Bee was renowned as being the noisiest establishment in Little Pletzl.

Take, for instance, the regular Tuesday morning group of five men. They had been coming to Zee Bee ever since the first day Zemel and Zlata had opened their doors. Always on a Tuesday morning. Always for two hours. Always the same breakfast. Two well-scrambled eggs, tomato, no cucumber, a toasted plain bagel, and a regular coffee. They had their favourite booth located at the back of the bakery, away from the regular clientele.

They were known discreetly by staff as the Little Pletzl Pishers Circle.

Like many individuals who have travelled through countless lands, I have come across many pishers in my time. Some big, some little. These particular pishers were right out of central casting.

Three of the Little Pletzl Pishers were members of the village council. Plotnick, Velvel, and Ackerman. In addition, Indyk the chief of police, with his dog Tookhas, and Khōu of Khōu Chinese Restaurant rounded the group off.

Today, the conversation centred on Little Pletzl's uninvited visitor. Twm who spoke Twm.

"We need to concentrate on a long-term plan of action," remarked Ackman, slurping his third cup of coffee. All five heads nodded in agreement. All eight eyes turned to Khōu.

"Nu, why are you all looking at me?"

"Because," replied Plotnick.

"Because what?" responded Khōu.

"Er hum! Do you mind if I say something?" said Indyk.

Indyk rarely said anything, other than the occasional "sit Tookhas" to his dog, who at that particular time, waited patiently for pieces of well-scrambled eggs to fall onto the floor.

"Well, Indyk, out with it! What dazzling idea do you have to say?" Velvel had such a nice way of expressing himself. He always received compliments for his enunciation.

"Yes! Well, just thinking allowed . . . the 25th of December is long-term. Right? The day most Frantsoydishers traditionally eat out at Khōu's Chinese Restaurant."

"And, and?" interrupted Plotnick.

"And what if Twm was alone for a few hours and someone, or some entities guided him out of the village."

"Entities? What entities?" asked Velvel.

"Okay, gentlemen. Keep me out of this entitiesshentities thing! Are you crazy? That's months away. Do you know how busy I'll be on December 25, with all the hordes of Frantsoydishers demanding, yelling they've waited too long for their order, or, they want the same booth as they sat in last year, or …"

It was Khōu who made a valid point.

"Okay, Khōu! For goodness sake. You've made your point," responded Ackerman.

Plotnick raised his eyebrows, denoting he had something to say.

"It's far too problematic. In any case, the goy Twm has a new-found friend. Yankele, the Mayor's son."

Ackerman also had something to share.

"As you know, I'm not a fan of the village's self-appointed guru, Gurdayal the Compassionate." All the pishers nodded in agreement. "But I remember him quoting Exodus 22:22. 'You shall not wrong nor oppress the stranger, for you were strangers in the Land of Egypt.'"

Disappointing as it was to the Little Pletzl Pishers Circle, to my knowledge, the idea was never spoken about again. ☼

18

GESHMAK Deli, owned by Metger, also doubles up as the butchers, dentist, and barbershop, a combination I have never quite come across before in all my flying days.

The deli part of the establishment was renowned for an ancient traditional Hungarian dish called Matkes, the formula of which was a long-held secret by the Metger family. By all accounts, Matkas contained a mixture of matzo balls and latkes.

Geshmak was a regular Sunday lunch meeting venue for Little Pletzl's elderly bizarre characters, all intent on finding a long-lasting loving relationship.

Let me try to explain. They had been there, and done it, but not with much success. Yet, they are still trying to live in the world of their youth. They feel they are ridiculed and judged unfairly by the Little Pletzl youth and therefore they take every opportunity, through their bizarre deeds and jesting, to show they have a standing in society. All their actions are overdone and repeated.

If any of the elderly characters had possessed one microscopic spark of theatrical talent, the famous Vilna Troupe of its day, I am sure, would have readily signed them up.

Take, for instance, Abe.

Abe has a minority ownership in Little Pletzl's broiler and layer chicken farm. He's an unappealing, poorly-dressed short, bald, pot-bellied, rotund, lisp-speaking, short-sighted womanizer, who's utterly concerned about his baldness. He constantly attempts to brush his thin strands of hair forward. He has a large growth of hair in his ears and nose. He flaunts himself in front of any woman willing to listen to his chicken stories. He regards himself as God's answer to all women, he falls in love with every woman he comes in contact with and he has an answer for everything and everyone.

His poorly-dressed stature is accentuated by a trailing large woolen scarf – never seen off of his neck – and a long oversize leather coat, with a fur collar. All of which he apparently wears throughout the year.

And then, there's Gitta.

Ah yes, Gitta! Married three times. All dead!

She's extremely tall, thin, attractive-looking in a sexy way, with drooping eyes, in her late 80s, with a deep loud voice, and a high-pitch laugh. She always wears a T-shirt inscribed with the words, "Women Powerful Together."

Generations ago her family made the voyage, more like an expedition, from Pest in Hungary to Little Pletzl. Gitta never ceased telling anyone, now of a diminishing group who would listen, that the men in her family joined as volunteers in the Pest national guard to fight the Croatians.

Gitta, over the years, somehow had acquired a pseudo-Hungarian-Frantsoydish strong accent, the likes of which in Little Pletzl remained exclusively with her.

She never acknowledged Abe, much to his irritation. After all, Abe was only a village chicken farmer and her family came from Hungary!

The third member of this colourful thespian troupe was non-other than Geshmak's assistant manager. Yossel, who constantly bellowed at everyone. In his youth, he had dreamed of being a poet. Not just an ordinary poet, but writing satirical prose. He revered Jewish-born Heinrich Heine, a distant cousin of Karl Marx.

Yossel's one major failure can be attributed to a prose he wrote about an older man taking a young wife. It commenced, "Az an alter man nemt a yiner veib, er vet yung un zee alt." *(When an old man takes a young wife, he becomes young and she old).*

Needless to say, there was an uproar! The president of The Little Pletzl Council of Frantsoydish Women (LPCFW), none other than Gitta, came out strongly against Yossel's attempted prose, even though he, with every bit of clarity he could muster, declared his work was satirical in nature and by no means offensive to women.

However, the name of Yossel was affirmed by the LPCFW as being persona non grata and he was subsequently banned forthwith from attending Little Pletzl literary events. Such was the power of the LPCFW.

The point is, from then on, dejected and full of remorse, Yossel never wrote again. ☼

19

NURSE Pesha was proud of her profession. As one of two Little Pletzl primary nurses, the other was her twin sister Frayda, she took her duties as a caregiver to her patients with the utmost concern. She fulfilled all the needs expected of her, ensuring Frantsoydisher patients were observed and monitored, receiving their medications to aid in their recovery, and so forth. Providing patient care was an integral part of who she was.

That is until she came in contact with Twm who spoke Twm.

For example, it first started with her inability to verbally communicate with Twm in Frantsoydish, which then expanded into family sign language, auxiliary sign language, and then manually coded language.

Even Dr. Christin Wójcik, a master scholar of the works of Charles-Michel de l'Épée, of Versailles, recognised as 'The Father of Humanity,' who laid the groundwork for the signed oral languages of today, was unable to have any resemblance of communication with Twm, who spoke Twm.

As Nurse Pesha, in a fit of frustration exclaimed, "Er kukt mit di oygn, hert mit di oyern, un farshteyt vi di vant!" *(He looks with his eyes, listens with his ears, and understands like a wall!).*

Dear reader, at this point, let us pause here from this depressing scenario and recap some earlier details I have mentioned, which you might recall.

ONE early typical Sunday spring morning, in the Village of Little Comely-on-the-Marsh, somewhere in the south of France, where an eccentric Welsh community had lived undetected for hundreds of years, the mist had hardly risen, and the delicious smell of the first Welsh paned o goffi, *(cup of coffee)* had still to be made, a young man by the name of Twm, the son of Mayor Hastings and Mildred, his wife, got on his bicycle and without the knowledge of Felicity his partner, headed out for the first time in his life, to explore the countryside.

He had a mission, to seek out the location of his friend Usman the Usman, the only friend he had ever had.

Before Usman returned to his home in Luc-en-Dios, he had whispered to Twm the vicinity of where he would be staying.

"If you can, find your way to Route D61. I'll be staying for a while at my aunt's cottage. It's located somewhere between La Charce and Rottier. I'm sure you can't miss it!"

Unfortunately for Twm, he missed it! En route, his bike skidded on the slippery road, and in ending up in a ditch, his right leg became entangled in the down tube of his bike.

THE conclusion of these details is important to this storyline.

Twm, by some means, ended up in Little Pletzl's Zelda and Motti Medical Centre, where he was diagnosed by Dr. Christin Wójcik as having transient global amnesia. Memory loss. And that was where Twm encountered the lovely Nurse Pesha's words. "Oh my god, he's, he's uncircumcised!"

Under the circumstances, one wouldn't have expected this outburst to lead to anything one might consider out of the ordinary. But, as in many things that happen in Little Pletzl, as ordinary creatures, you and I are completely mystified as to the finer points that occur by its village residents.

Take, for instance, Nurse Pesha. She was not a commonplace nurse. In her life, outside the nursing profession, she had one goal. To make her mark as an accomplished glyph artist.

It was Dr. Christin Wójcik who was first taken with Nurse Pesha's extraordinary non-professional ability to freely express herself. He suggested she overcome any obstacles she had with Twm's physical feature, by taking him, in his wheelchair, for a stroll around the village.

"Show him the highlight spots in the village," he said. He added, with a smile, "Perhaps Twm's new-found friend, Yankele, the son of Mayor Sandek, and Mrs. Blume might also want to join you".

In addition, he proposed Nurse Pesha consider creating a commission piece of glyth for the entrance of the Medical Centre. But first, she corrected the Doctor.

"Dr. Wójcik, there's quite a difference between a "glyph" and a "glyth."

"Is there?" he responded, with a look that

showed he had no idea what she was talking about.

Nurse Pesha looked at him. "Oh, Doctor, you're so silly! You must know a glyth, that's with a tee and an aich, is a ringed planet approximately 600,000,000 kilometers from the sun, and one day lasts over 30 hours."

She paused. "I'm a glyph artist, that's a glyph with a pee aich."

To be honest, I've no idea where this is leading. However, in any event, she readily agreed to the commission, for up to now, her works had been dismissed by the Village Council and the administrators of the Zena and Motti Foundation as having no style.

IN leaving the Medical Centre, within a short time, the language barrier between Twm, Yankele, and Nurse Pesha put none of them off, for it showed again, with credible evidence, obstacles can be overcome.

In the meantime, watching the three together, meandering through the pathways of Little Pletzl was a sight to see. Yankele, who had been diagnosed as a socially anxious introvert, for the first time in his life had finally found a real friend in Twm, who spoke

Twm. Twm, who was diagnosed as having transient global amnesia, and Nurse Pesha, a frustrated glyph artist, were the perfect trifecta of oddballs supreme.

I do not mean to suggest for an instant they were any different from the majority of Little Pletzlers, god forbid. However, as they approached the edge of the Little Pletzl pond with its warty-faced Muscovy Ducks vying for their attention, they were joined by none other than the self-proclaimed orthodox Jewish guru, Gurdayal the Compassionate, the spiritual vegan advisor and mentor to the youth of the village, who had by now not only decided to drop his Frantsoydish name, Yitzhak, but had also, now approaching his 92nd birthday, with one of the best Jewish law and jurisprudence minds in the village, who knew everything there was to know about Halakha, decided to renounce his volunteer title as der anderer rebbe, *(the other rabbi)*.

For Twm, all of this fresh air, the familiar pond, the surrounding forest, and the feeling he recognized Gurdayal the Compassionate from another place, left him confused. Even Nurse Pesha's actions seemed somewhat familiar to him. However, he dismissed it all as a by-product of his memory loss. And as for Yankele, other than Yankele having blond hair and blue eyes and he having red hair, freckles and brown eyes, Yankele's actions were the spitting image of his at an earlier stage in his life.

MOST of this had not gone unnoticed by Indyk, Little Pletzl's chief of police, and his dog Tookhas. And as the longstanding regulations governing foreigners specified, he reported the event to the Little Pletzl Police Services Board's Chair, none other than Blume, the wife of Mayor Sandek.

In response to further questioning by the Chair, Indyk admitted that after discreetly following the four in question, he observed them at the edge of the Pletzl pond laughing and allegedly talking quietly to the warty-faced Muscovy Ducks.

The Chair insisted on knowing what they were talking about, to which Indyk responded that their backs were facing him and he was too far away to hear their alleged conversation. In any case, he couldn't speak Twm, could he? However, for the record, he had written down in his notebook the warty-faced Muscovy Ducks were wagging their tails out of joy!

Dear reader, Blume's response was not unexpected. To use one's creative imagination in what happened thereafter, might well prepare you for the consequences.

"Oy-yoy-yoy! Shanda fur die goyim! Loz mikh aleyn!" *(A shame before the nations. Leave me alone)*, Blume shrieked, melodramatically raising both of her hands over her heart.

There's nothing finer than an opera-staged drama taking place without a musical score. There's no doubt, this came very close to being one, featuring as the diva, Blume, aka the Norse woman Lagertha, aka Little Pletzl's Police Services Board's Chair, and wife of Mayor Sandek.

It was a scene of the diva, in her thoughts, seeing in front of her what she believed was the slow demise of Yankele, her socially anxious introvert son.

For Blume, she had heard her son, who never spoke to her, was not only gallivanting around the village with a non-Jew, but he was also allegedly talking to the ducks! The combination was too empathetically painful for her. It was, in her eyes, a personal embarrassment for her family and the community. For her, a shanda is an embarrassing behaviour by a Jew in front of a Gentile. ☼

20

BLUME'S inharmonious shriek made even the most religious stalwart of Little Pletzl's community wonder if Hashem *(Messiah)* had finally arrived.

At the time of Blume's outburst, perhaps it was just as well that Rabbi Dudel was out for his afternoon stroll, walking in the direction of the Shenken distillery. Many of its older patrons, all with a glass of something in their hand, had already taken their position outside of Shenken's front door, facing the pond, waiting for their rebbe, who was seen walking as fast as he could, in support of many of his beloved congregation towards them. Past the Little Pletzl Pipdówka Shul. Past the Zelda and Motti Playhouse. Past the Zelda and Motti Pökelpiłka Sports Park, where the Little Pletzl Pökelpiłka

Players Association played Pökelpiłka.

And dear reader, approaching from the opposite direction, near the Zelda and Motti Medical Centre, Gurdayal the Compassionate, the self-proclaimed orthodox Jewish guru, the spiritual vegan advisor and mentor to the youth of the village, decked out in his white clothing, comprising of upper and lower garments with sandals, with his long grey hair flowing in the wind, and a pure white yarmulke adorning his head, had excused himself from being with Nurse Pesha, Twm who spoke Twm and Yankele. For now, he hastily headed to be with many of his young congregation as they eagerly waited for him at the Shenken distillery.

In addition, to round off this auspicious event, on the other side of the Little Pletzl pond, all the customers from Geshmak Deli, Khōu Chinese Restaurant, Potchke Restaurant and Tea Rooms, and Zemel's Bakery had congregated on the far eastern corner of the Little Pletzl Pond, to watch this event come into being.

Not to be outdone, the Muscovy Ducks, joined by the Canada Geese, sensing something of great importance was about to happen, positioned themselves in the centre of the pond.

It all had the makings of a cultural standoff.

DR. Christin Wójcik sauntered over to join Nurse Pesha, Yankele, and Twm the Twm who spoke Twm.

"Oh Dr. Wójcik," Nurse Pesha said. "I have no idea what's happening, but I now have a wonderful idea for my commission piece for the Medical Centre."

She pointed at all the people emerging in groups surrounding the pond.

"Just look, a hieroglyph is forming in front of us!"

"Mae hieroglyff? Hieroglyff? Rwy'n gwybod y gair hwnnw!" *(A hieroglyph? I know that word!)* Twm had finally spoken, in Welsh, his language. He had found one common word they all understood.

There was added surprise, this time from Yankele.

"Dr. Christin Wójcik, you and your family were once outsiders, but eventually accepted into the community. What do our people have against Twm?"

"Yankele, some things are very hard to figure out." He paused, smiled, and continued.

"I believe it was Plato, the Greek philosopher who said: 'We can easily forgive a child who is afraid of the dark; the real tragedy of life is when men are afraid of the dark.'

"Let me tell you something. Our village, Little Pletzl has been regarded by our community as being isolated from the rest of the world. Generations ago our people who came here from many lands, wanted it this way. Group by group, community by community, they decided they'd had enough of the social order they were living under. So, they moved west, seeking out an area of autonomous land where they would be left alone to continue doing whatever Frantsoydisher Jews do best. So far, it's been a good existence. We're self-sufficient in every way. Our surroundings are clean and healthy. And Little Pletzl is encircled by a dense forest containing incredible thick vegetation which acts as our security blanket."

The doctor looked at Twm.

"And then comes along this handsome young man with red hair, freckles, and brown eyes, we believe is called Twm. His facial features and mannerisms are different from ours. He's an outsider. He doesn't speak Frantsoydish, our language. We haven't any idea what his language is, or where he came from. Do you and Pesha understand? Look around you. In just a few days since his arrival, our community is being swept up in internal conflict. Our community is afraid of him. For his own sake and ours, he must leave as soon as possible." ☼

21

THE next day, Mayor Sandek issued a call of action to his village council to come together again to help lessen the damage caused by the uninvited stranger. Twm.

Chef Glucke, the wife of the late Michelin Chef Nahum, was instructed to prepare an early morning breakfast at the Potchke Restaurant and Tea Rooms, the village's kosher 1-star Michelin establishment. The meeting will be in camera.

"So, Sandek, what's your Blume been up to?" It was Plotnick who first opened up the subject.

They were all there, sitting around the table. Gurdayal the Compassionate, Plotnick in charge of buildings, Shprintza, the business manager, Velvel, finance, Health & Welfare, and Ackerman, agriculture.

Sandek just sat there, preoccupied. "So, Sandek, what's your Blume been up to?" Plotnick repeated.

The Mayor slowly turned towards them all, one by one, taking time to pause at each of them. It was Ackerman who ventured further.

"Er klert tsi a floy hot a pupik!" *(He's meditating on whether a flea has a belly button)*.

With that, Mayor Sandek got up and walked out of the meeting.

"What did I say?" asked Ackerman, as he wiped away the last vestiges of black bread from his mouth.

"And Velvel, don't start up! This isn't the time for your role in Wagner's Die Meistersinger von Nürnberg."

Dear reader, to you, this all might seem so amusing and dramatic compared to your mundane life. However, for those present, they believed the issue at hand was one of importance, the future of their community, their village, Little Pletzl-on-the-Zump. If I might use a personal expression, this issue will not fly away.

After some minutes had passed, Mayor Sandek returned to the meeting where his council members waited patiently to hear what he had to say.

Dramatic as it all seems followed. Before the Mayor had time to open his mouth, all eyes moved away from him to focus on the door of their dining room.

"Gut morgen, tate!" *(Good morning, Dad!)*

Yankele, the youngest son of Sandek, entered from the shadows. Hidden from view was Twm.

"Tate! Dos bin ikh, dayn zun Yankele." *(Daddy! It's me, your son Yankele).*

Yankele stepped forward, directly in front of Sandek, he smiled with tears in his eyes, and extended his arms waiting for a response from his father. None came.

LATER that day, the members of the village council were still talking about what happened, about the difficulty Mayor Sandek had in expressing a remark to his son.

To be sure, nothing could have prepared Sandek to listen to his son speak for the first time. For Yankele, a physically fragile young man, yet intellectually gifted, who, before he had met Twm, had never spoken to another human, and for all of his 19 years had been deprived of emotional support from his parents, nothing came close to what he had experienced a few hours earlier.

And for Twm, the morning's incident had shaken him to the core. He had personally suffered through a similar event before, with his father, the Mayor of Little Comely-on-the-Marsh. He knew it in Welsh as "*Eisoes wedi'i brofi*." You, dear reader, might know it by the French term, "*déjà éprouvé*".☼

22

IT was Nurse Frayda who broke the news to Dr. Wójcik. The doctor, in his spare time, was an amateur ornithologist, and on that particular early Sunday spring morning in the forest behind the Zelda and Motti Medical Centre, he had set his sights on finding the whereabouts of the short-toed treecreeper, not, I will add, to be confused with the common treecreeper. Using my knowledge of this particular species, as one might expect, the short-toed treecreeper has shorter toes than the common treecreeper.

It is a known fact that short-toed nests are in tree crevices or behind bark flakes and this is where the doctor was focusing his interest that is until Nurse Frayda found him.

"Ah, Frayda, look over there. You have better eyesight than I do." He pointed above to a nest made of twigs, pine needles, and bark. "Do those eggs have purple-red blotches on them?"

Nurse Frayda was in no mood to help out. "Dr. Wójcik, please. We have a problem back at the medical centre. It's my twin sister Pesha. You better come immediately!"

By the time they arrived back at the medical centre, Pesha, with a big smile on her face, was waiting for them with her hieroglyphics. So was Gurdayal the Compassionate.

She had indeed followed Dr. Wójcik's instructions as to what wall she could use, the colour, and the theme, well possibly not exactly the theme. As she enthusiastically pointed out to him, "Yes, look over there." Painted on the wall facing Dr. Wójcik's office, she had used Ankh the Egyptian symbol of life, as the primary theme. That was a given. However, she had taken the matter a stage further by exploring various other comparable symbols as she remarked, "Were to recognize one's personal sensations."

One huge symbolic design, painted on the wall facing the medical centre's entrance, involved the ancient Egyptian symbol of Tjet, the symbol for the female reproductive organs, and the goddess Isis in her role as the universal mother.

Dr. Wójcik stepped back, sighed, and turned towards Gurdayal the Compassionate.

"Yitzhak, I'm glad you're here. Do you have a few minutes? There's something I want to talk to you about."

As Nurse Frayda looked on in silence, one could hear in the forest the trill of the short-toed treecreeper. "Tweetutwee-too-tititit … Tweetutwee-too-tititit!" ☼

23

WEDNESDAY is Market Day in Little Pletzl. Many years ago the village elders decreed that tradition and the way of life, as it was in their old countries, should continue at least one day a week. A market would bring a strong Frantsoydisher feeling to the community.

Originally, a site just north of where the Little Pletzl Pökelpiłka Players Association play Pökelpiłka, and where the Little Pletzl Pipdówka Shul is now located, was selected. Unfortunately, at that time, in their enthusiasm, the elders didn't take into account that the area was not only saturated with a marsh, but it was also a breeding area for the Muscovy Ducks.

"Es is a zump!" *(It is a marsh!)*, the cry went out.

And so an alternative site was agreed upon, located on the south side of the Little Pletzl pond, between where the Zelda and Motti Medical Centre and Zemel's Bakery are today.

TO return to Yankele and his friend Twm. It was early Wednesday morning. The previous evening Little Pletzl had been subjected to a torrential storm, which bears no relevance to this story. However, the morning was misty and damp and Twm, who now had back most of his memory faculties, recognised the weather as comparable to that of Little Comely-on-the-Marsh.

As he looked around he noticed some similarities with his village market. Many stall owners were setting up their produce and goods, all of which looked as if they were taken right out of Little Comely. And for those stall owners who had arrived at the crack of dawn, they were already selling their produce, eggs, and chickens.

In Little Comely, the market faced the Duke of Wellington pub, which was constantly full of his Welsh male and female neighbours drinking their favourite warm Welsh beer. Here, in Little Pletzl, Shenken's distillery, which he could just see through the mist, seemed remote from the market.

Twm's full memory had returned, but he hadn't fully recuperated from his bicycle accident and he was still confined by Dr. Wójcik to his wheelchair.

Dr. Wójcik had now given the task of pushing Twm to Yankele. Nurse Pesha, much to her shock, as instructed by the doctor, was busy removing all her hieroglyphics from the walls of the Zena and Motti Medical Centre.

Yankele tried his best to set some market ground rules for Twm using sign language, such as don't pick up a dead chicken and start plucking it. However, Twm was more interested in tasting some of the traditional Frantsoydish dishes offered to him. Knish, kugel, and babka filled with cinnamon and chocolate were amongst his favourites. The smallest portion of gefilte fish, topped with a slice of carrot, was rejected outright.

WHILE all of this was happening, at the insistence of Blume, the Chair of the Little Pletzl Police Services Board, Mayor Sandek called for a casual lunch meeting of the Village Council. This time they met in a back room of the Shenken distillery, facing the Canada Geese.

A dairy lunch catered by Zemel's Bakery consisted of cabbage soup, stuffed peppers, hardboiled eggs, potato latkes, cheese blintzes, and spinach salad. Pletzl bread sprinkled with cooked onions and poppy seeds and hot black tea added to the order.

Police Chief Indyk also attended the lunch. His dog Tookhas sat outside gazing at the Canada Geese, while several pigeons on the roof of the Shenken, including the Carneau, Crested Soultz, French Mondain, and the common rock pigeon, stared down at Tookhas.

"Right, Sandek we need an Ep," insisted Shprintza.

Sandek looked confused. "An Ep?"

"An entry point in which to find an excuse to get rid of the goy."

"Do you mind if I say something?" It was Gurdayal the Compassionate.

"Yes, we do mind, so why don't you ..."

"Now, now Ackerman, calm down. Let's hear what he has to say," exclaimed Sandek.

Gurdayal the Compassionate stood up and cleared his throat.

"Well, it's not as simple as you might think.

115

Actually, it's quite complex and challenging."

Dear reader, if I might butt in. Gurdayal the Compassionate's whole posture had changed back from being a Jewish Guru to that of Yitzhak, der anderer rebbe, a very deaf 91-year-old, with one of the best Jewish law and jurisprudence minds in the village, who knew everything there was to know about Halakha, the laws derived from the written and Oral Torah, but nothing about deportation matters, as you will now read.

"Legally, of course, I am not an expert on a deportation order, but I ask you, has this man Twm conspired to commit a crime or fraudulent act while here? Is he a French citizen? Who is he? Where was he born? How and why did he arrive here? Has he claimed refugee status in Little Pletzl? Has he asked us for protection? …"

"Yitzhak, please enough already!"

The Mayor raised his right hand, palm extended.

"Talking on behalf of my friends around the table, none of us are interested, Yitzhak, in your legal interpretation and questions regarding the goy. We just want to get rid of him. He's simply not one of us, right?

"Hold on a minute! Sandek," Plotnick shouted,

"What do you mean by you want to get rid of him?" "Du farkirtst mir di yorn!" (*You'll be the death of me!*).

Ackerman couldn't resist joining in. "Plotnick, nem zich a vaneh! *(Go jump in the lake!).*

Plotnick turned red and got up as if he was going to attack Ackerman. "Khazer!" *(Pig!).*

"Khamer!" *(Donkey!)* countered Ackerman.

"Momzer!" *(A child born out of wedlock)* replied Plotnick.

Mayor Sandek looked at Yitzhak. "Yitzhak, please take over running the meeting from me, I'm going out for some fresh air."

Yitzhak nodded. "Then you better take the front door, unless you want to step in some Canada Geese' shit!"

Mayor Sandek sighed. "There's enough of that in this room!"

SOMETIME later Mayor Sandek returned to the meeting shaken at what had happened.

"What have I missed? Anything I should know about?"

Shprintza offered an answer. "Nothing at all, Sandek. We were just talking about our delicious catered lunch from Zemel's Bakery, especially the Pletzl bread."

All this time, throughout all of the emotional outbursts, Indyk sat there quietly observing the situation. Even his police dog Tookhas had remained, as instructed, outside the back door, gazing at the Canada Geese.

Mayor Sandek looked at Indyk. "Well, Indyk, what have you to say?"

Indyk stood up, excused himself, and as he calmly walked out said, "Yes, I do have something brief to say. You're all acting like a bunch of quangos!" ☼

24

LATER in the evening Gurdayal, the Compassionate, and Dr. Christin Wójcik shared their plan with Nurse Frayda. The plan was devised to spirit Twm home to his family.

On Sunday morning at sunrise, she and Yankele were to bring Twm to the spot in the forest where the doctor had set his sights on finding the whereabouts of the short-toed treecreeper. He would meet them there.

"And what if Yankele wants to join Twm?" asked Nurse Frayda.

The Doctor smiled softly, "Let's bridge that problem when and if it comes up."

IT was another typical Little Pletzl Sunday spring morning. The mist had hardly risen amongst the pine, oak, and beech trees. Even the short-toed treecreeper hadn't yet accepted the start of the day.

Dr. Wójcik was waiting for them. Nurse Frayda and Twm were accompanied by Yankele. As the three approached the doctor, they observed him talking to a man they didn't recognise. The alarm turned to bewilderment.

"Frayda, Yankele, Twm, come over here. I believe you know this man. You may know him as either Gurdayal the Compassionate or as Yitzhak der anderer rebbe and lawyer. I know him by his real name, Isaac of Little Comely."

Isaac approached the three. He extended his hand to Twm.

"Helo, Twm! Ydych chi'n cofio fi? Fe af â chi adref nawr. Mae Felicity yn aros amdanoch chi." *(Hello, Twm. Do you remember me? I will take you home now. Felicity is waiting for you).*

Twm was overwhelmed having heard Welsh, his native language, spoken by Isaac.

"Shalom Frayda. Shalom Yankele. Did I surprise you?"

He was hardly recognizable. Gone was his self-proclaimed orthodox Jewish guru appearance, his white clothing, comprising of upper and lower garments with open sandals, and his white yarmulke. He even had cut his flowing shoulder-length grey hair.

It was Yankele who stepped forward. He pointed to Isaac.

"Er ken makhn dem kholem greser vi di nakht." *(He can make the dream larger than night).*

Dr. Christin Wójcik turned to Twm and Yankele. "Yankele, Isaac will be joining you. Follow him and he will lead you and Twm to an opening in the forest where you can safely walk to Little Comely. Afterwards, Isaac will return here to Little Pletzl, his family home."

Yankele turned towards the doctor. "But Dr. Wójcik, I'm not going with Twm. I'm staying here, in Little Pletzl." Nurse Frayda looked at the doctor and with a tight-lipped grin nodded at him.

"So, now, it's time for our goodbyes," remarked the doctor. He approached Twm and hugged him. "Shalom, my young friend. Biz hundert un tsvantsig." *(May you live to be 120 years old)* Isaac translated it into Welsh for Twm.

Twm looked at Dr. Christin Wójcik and laughed.

"Genesis 6:3." He added, "Rwyt ti i gyd yn frodyr a chwiorydd i mi. Diolch!" *(You are all my brothers and sisters. Thank you!)*.

THE spring sun's rays had finally broken through the mist as Dr. Christin Wójcik and Nurse Frayda walked back to Little Pletzl's Zena and Motti Medical Centre.

"Dr. Wójcik, I have hundreds of questions to ask you and ..."

He put his hand on her shoulder. "Yes, in time, I promise." He looked up towards a tree where a short-toed treecreeper was perched.

"Ah, Frayda, look over there. You have better eyesight than I do." He pointed above to a nest made of twigs, pine needles, and bark. "Do those eggs have purple-red blotches on them?" ☼☼

ABOUT THE AUTHOR

Alan L. Simons is an author, writer, and social advocate. He was born and educated in London, England, where he worked for various newspapers before immigrating to Canada. As a diplomat, he served as the Honorary Consul of the Republic of Rwanda to Canada, in the post-genocide era. He lectures and writes on issues relating to religion in politics, antisemitism, intolerance, hate, Islamophobia, conflict, and terrorism. The Village of Little Pletzl-on-the-Zump is his sixth published book.

Other Books by Alan L. Simons

EIGHTEEN MONTHS-A LOVE STORY INTERRUPTED

A story of a human relationship that testifies to the strength and will of both the terminally ill patient and her partner as he comes to accept her illness and the short period of time they will spend together.

THE VILLAGE OF LITTLE COMELY-ON-THE-MARSH

This hilarious and satirical story weaves around the lives of an eccentric Welsh community living in a small village somewhere in the south of France exclusively in their own sheltered world.

THE CHILDREN OF THE FOREST

Written for both grown-ups and older children. Loosely based on a story by Rabbi Nahman of Bratslav. A folktale in the European tradition. Kabbalistic, Mystical, Esoteric, Freygish. An account of two Polish Jewish children from pre-teens to adulthood, together with five mystical characters and Klezmer musicians.

THE INCREDIBLE ADVENTURES OF CAPTAIN MACDUDDYFUNK IN CUGGERMUGGERLAND

The children of Canada's Minister of Missing Islands, are magically transported to the mysterious island of Cuggermuggerland where they meet the Quidnuncs, who love to hug, and the Shilpits, who always scream and shout at each other.

SWEATY CATS AND BABY PIGEONS

A series of short stories written for the inquiring mind of a young child, in which grandparents can interact and stimulate communication between the generations.

https://alanlsimons.wordpress.com/